D0286161

A Novel Idea

AIMEE FRIEDMAN

Simon Pulse
New York London Toronto Sydney

For my mom
who loves books, too
And with thanks to Bethany Buck—mentor, editor, friend

SIMON PULSE
An imprint of Simon & Schuster
Children's Publishing Division
1230 Avenue of the Americas
New York, NY 10020
Copyright © 2006 by Aimee Friedman
All rights reserved, including the right of reproduction in
whole or in part in any form.
SIMON PULSE and colophon are registered trademarks of
Simon & Schuster, Inc.
Designed by Ann Zeak
The text of this book was set in Garamond 3.
Manufactured in the United States of America
First Simon Pulse edition January 2006
10 9 8 7 6 5 4 3 2 1
Library of Congress Control Number 2005928862
ISBN-13: 978-1-4169-0785-5
ISBN-10: 1-4169-0785-8

Sometimes truth is stranger than fiction.
—Bad Religion, "Stranger Than Fiction"

They say life is the thing, but I prefer reading.
—Logan Pearsall Smith

One

I'm not a hopeless romantic. I don't believe in love at first sight or destiny or soul mates. I'm happiest wearing a charcoal zip-up hoodie and vintage jeans, not some floaty pastel dress with kitten-heeled mules. I hate bouquets of roses, boxes of chocolate, and Jessica Simpson ballads. And most of all, I despise Valentine's Day.

February fourteen of my junior year was especially rough. The halls of my high school, Edna St. Vincent Millay, were decorated with heart-shaped pink balloons and tacky plastic cupids. I spent the day skirting cuddly couples kissing against lockers and giggly girls carrying heaps of carnations. By the time I arrived for my three o'clock meeting with Ms. Bliss, the college counselor, I was beat.

"Norah Bloom." Ms. Bliss greeted me, flashing a grin as she glanced up from a file on her desk. She had wavy blond hair, a pert nose, and, under her prim lavender suit, an ultra-curvy figure. I remembered the rumor my friend Scott Harper had told me earlier that year—that Ms. Bliss was an undercover Victoria's Secret model sent to our high school to terrorize insecure teenage girls. Maybe it was true; already I felt way too pale, dark-haired, and flat-chested in her presence.

"Hey," I muttered. I flopped in a chair across from her and stared down at my orange Pumas. The fluorescent office lights buzzed rudely.

"Norah, I am *so* sorry to keep you after school on a holiday," Ms. Bliss began, crossing her long legs and tapping a French-manicured nail on a sheet of paper. "I'm sure you have plans tonight, like me."

Instantly, my eyes shot to the wooden frame on Ms. Bliss's desk, which held a photo of a square-jawed possible gym trainer.

"Not really," I said. My Valentine's plan was: meet my best friend, Audre Legrand, for coffee at the Book Nook, endure dinner with my family, and slink off to my room to reread my tattered copy of *Weetzie Bat*, blast my Postal Service CD, and ignore my homework.

Sexy, huh?

"Oh, that's too bad," Ms. Bliss purred, her glossy lips curling up in a smug smile. "But let's jump right in, shall we? Since second semester started in January, I've been meeting individually with each junior to discuss his or her college goals."

I sat up straighter, brushing my bangs off my forehead. College. I couldn't freaking *wait*. I was dying for sunny green campuses, cozy library stacks, and noisy freshman dorms. I wanted to stay up all night with my roommates, eating cold pizza and arguing about the meaning of life. In college, I was sure, the stresses of high school—popularity and acne and standardized tests—would disappear. And in college I might meet a poetic, dark-eyed philosophy major who, unlike every other boy in the world, would finally *notice* me.

"Where do I start?" I asked excitedly, practically bursting out of my seat. Ms. Bliss, clearly startled by my sudden spike in energy, leaned back in her swivel chair with a tiny gasp. "I have *such* college goals, Ms. Bliss," I went on breathlessly. "I mean, my friends and I all feel like we've, I don't know, *outgrown* high school or something. I want"—I paused, searching for just the right phrase. Audre always teases me about being a stickler for words—"time away from my parents, and amazing classes that will flip my world upside down and—"*A boyfriend*, I wanted to add. But, thankfully, didn't.

"I've even checked out some schools' Web sites," I said instead, "like, Sarah Lawrence and Vassar—"

"That's all very well and good, Norah." Ms. Bliss cut me off, her eyes skimming down what appeared to be my report card. "However." She glanced back up at me and shook her head in disappointment.

I bit my lip and adjusted my cat-eyed, tortoiseshell glasses, trying to look serious and academic. My palms were turning clammy. *However* what? As far as I remembered, my grades—especially in English and history—were pretty good. Okay, maybe my C plus in chemistry didn't make my GPA glitter, but I hadn't said I was shooting for Harvard.

"Uh, did I do something wrong?" I managed to ask, my voice—to my horror—coming out in a squeak. My problem is, I get embarrassed too easily, by pretty much anything I do. I'm less painfully shy than I was back in grade school, when talking to anyone other than Audre would cause me to break out in hives. But I'm still pretty bad.

"I have one word for you, dear." Ms. Bliss grinned again to show how well her Crest Whitestrips were working. "Extracurriculars."

"Extracurriculars?" I repeated, my stomach sinking. I knew that after-school activities were super-important to colleges —Millay students had that drilled into their brains starting in freshman year. And I'd tried. It wasn't my fault that I got kicked off the girls' volleyball team after one day. (Apparently, being able to serve over the net is really, really important.) And it wasn't like I'd *planned* to pass out over the frog guts when my mom hooked

5

me up with a volunteer job at her research lab. So by junior year I was seriously lacking in the activities department. I was about to explain myself, until, with a burst of relief, I remembered my stint at Millay's literary magazine.

"*Blank Canvas*!" I exclaimed, my face flushing in triumph. "I joined in September and edited some stories—"

"Seems you were a member for only a few months," Ms. Bliss interrupted.

How did she know *that*? Sometimes I wonder if school guidance counselors have a direct line to the CIA.

"The poems sucked," I replied with a sigh. "There was this one I had to edit that was called 'The Scent of My Agony.' I swear. I think that put me over the edge." *That*, I recalled, *and my unrequited crush on Seamus Higgins, the hot but asshole-ish editor in chief.*

Ms. Bliss sighed too. "Norah, colleges aren't going to care about excuses. They want to see commitment and initiative. So, starting this semester, I'd advise you to get busy."

I tensed up, paranoid that the all-knowing Ms. Bliss somehow was aware that I had never "gotten busy" in that *other* sense.

"Join the yearbook, the school paper, the photography club," she went on, fixing her ice-blue eyes on me. "Or start your own club—but with a teacher's permission, of course." She extended a finger toward my midsection and I drew in a breath, feeling like I was under attack. "Just get some extracurriculars under that faux-diamond-studded belt . . . or you can forget about Vassar."

Ouch. Instinctively, my hands flew to my favorite Urban Outfitters belt as if to shield myself, but it was too late. Ms. Bliss's remark had hit her target.

"I'll try?" I mumbled, unsure what else to say.

Ms. Bliss beamed, as if she hadn't spent the last few minutes tearing me to shreds. "Terrific," she chirped, and wriggled up out of her chair, a sign that I was to follow. She scribbled a date in May on a Post-it and handed it to me. "Best of luck to you, dear. Let's meet again at the end of the year to reassess."

I nodded and dragged myself out the door, fighting down the lump in my throat. The halls were empty of students now, but the cupids and balloons still floated forlornly around.

"Oh, and Norah?" Ms. Bliss called out from behind me. "Happy Valentine's Day."

The weather outside matched my mood. Sideways sleet hammered down from an angry gray sky, and Christopher Street was slick with ice. Yanking on my hood and jamming my hands into the pockets of my denim jacket, I tried to forget my Bliss-induced misery and concentrate on making my way to West 4th Street. A block ahead of me, Plum Anderson, the girl in my grade with the shiniest hair (extracurricular activities: shopping and sex) skidded in her furry mukluks and did the crazed I-don't-want-to-fall dance that everyone—even Plum Anderson—looks ridiculous doing. That cheered me up a little.

Millay is in New York City's Greenwich Village, which is home to lots of girls Audre and I like to call "Plums"—model-skinny types who chain-smoke and hide under tweed newsboy caps and oversized shades as if they're actual celebs. I feel lucky to live outside Manhattan, in the mellow, funky neighborhood of Park Slope, Brooklyn, where there is a very nice absence of Plums. Every afternoon, I catch the F train at the West 4th subway station and ride it all the way downtown, under the Manhattan Bridge, and into Brooklyn. The whole trip takes about half an hour, but the time goes quickly if I'm gossiping with Audre or reading a good book. And it's worth it. I love Park Slope; even though it's an urban neighborhood, its indie bookstores, boutiques, and cafés give it a small-town vibe.

That afternoon, I was more eager than ever to swipe my MetroCard, hurry down to the platform, and board the cramped train. As we bounced and swerved along the track, I gazed at the ads lining the car, wondering if any might give me an idea for my missing extracurricular activity. Most of them were for roach motels or aftershave—not that inspiring. Then I noticed the couple standing under the roach motel ad. They looked around my age, or maybe seventeen. The boy had spiky black hair and was bending down to kiss his scarlet-haired, punkette girlfriend. She was standing on her tiptoes, arms wrapped around his neck. From her left hand swung a paper cone of bright red tulips. Great. Even on the subway I couldn't avoid Valentine's Day.

"Get a room," I said under my breath, but I kept watching them. She must have been thanking him for the flowers. Maybe they were going out for a candlelit dinner later. Now his hands were in her hair as their kiss deepened. I was so focused on the couple that I gave a start when the train pulled into my station. *Whatever,* I thought, turning away. That kind of stuff doesn't get to me. Like I said, I'm not a hopeless romantic. Not at all.

When I got to the Book Nook, I spotted Audre sitting on a plump sofa in the back, pretending to knit a scarf. What she was really doing, of course, was checking out Griffin McCarthy, the hottie who works at the register.

Audre and I are obsessed with the Book Nook, and not only because of Griffin. It's this adorable bookstore that's right between our houses. The air smells of fresh coffee beans and the best music is always playing in the background. Today, the Pixies were serenading us. In the front of the store, where I was wringing the rain out of my low ponytail, are rows of shelves spilling over with a crazy mix of paperbacks and hardcovers. The owner's ink-black cats, who are all named after famous authors, roam around on the bright orange-and-blue rugs. In the back is a small café full of squishy chairs and couches where people sip vanilla cappuccinos and click away on their laptops. Actual writers hang there; I always hoped I would run into Philippa Askance, this Brooklyn punk poetess I worship, but I hadn't yet.

"You survived," Audre said as I plopped down beside her. She moved her knitting needles and tangle of yellow yarn aside, then pecked my cheek.

"You changed," I said, gesturing to her outfit.

To school that day, Audre had worn skinny cords, a purple cowl-neck, and her leopard-print flats. Now she was wearing an off-the-shoulder striped shirt and denim mini over fishnets and fuzzy boots. Her hair was pulled back in a curly dark pouf, big gold hoops dangled from her ears, and the shimmery blush on her cheekbones turned her cocoa-colored skin all glowy. It was obvious she'd made the special effort for Griffin. He doesn't work at the Book Nook every afternoon, but Audre has his schedule tacked up on the wall in her bedroom so she knows when she'll see him.

I'm serious.

"What's your point?" Audre grinned as she ran her pinkie over her full, glossy bottom lip.

"That you did *not* come here to knit," I teased. "Have you talked to him yet?" I turned to look at the register, where I'd seen Griffin a second before. Another guy was now in his place, so I glanced toward the coffee counter, where a tattooed girl was tending to some customers. "Hey, Aud, where'd your loverboy go—"

"Norah, Audre. What's up?" There was no mistaking that deep, slow-as-honey voice. I looked behind me, feeling my cheeks redden. There stood the loverboy in question, holding two steaming mugs and smiling at us from under his mop of shaggy golden hair.

"Griffin!" Audre and I exclaimed at the same instant, then looked at each other and burst into giggles.

Hello, mortification. My name is Norah. Perhaps we've met before?

Griffin didn't seem to notice our girly reaction. He simply set the mugs on the table in front of us and stretched his six-foot surfer's frame into a chair across from us.

"Two lattes, extra foam. Am I right?" he asked, winking at Audre as he toyed with the shell choker around his neck. Griffin isn't really my type—the blond California thing doesn't do it for me—but he still makes my pulse quicken and, like all boys, totally ties my tongue. It doesn't help that he's a freshman at New York University, so I'm forever wanting to ask him for the inside scoop on college—but I'm usually too nervous. I figure he wouldn't bother giving advice to a random high school junior.

"Well, we come here enough," Audre replied, cool as ever. She is forever poised, even in front of boys she likes. I watched as she lifted one of the mugs and took a long sip, then closed her eyes and tipped her head to one side, getting into what I call her Gourmet Diva Mode. "Mmm. Hazelnut infusion," she said approvingly.

I sipped the hot, foamy drink. All I tasted was milk and coffee. But that is the difference between Audre and me. Or, actually, between Audre and most high school kids. My best friend already has her life pretty much mapped out: She wants to go to cooking school and become a total domestic goddess, with her own line of pastry cookbooks and a television show—the African-American Nigella Lawson. Meanwhile, I have no idea what I want out of the future—except college. And now even that seemed like a giant question mark.

"Gracias." Griffin gave Audre a slow grin. "Just brewed 'em myself." The tattooed girl from the coffee counter wiggled past Griffin on her way to the front of the store, and I noticed that he followed her with his eyes.

"Aren't you supposed to work the register?" Audre asked, fluttering her lashes at him. It kills me that my best friend knows how to flirt without ever, to my knowledge, having taken any lessons.

"I've got a sweet deal with Patrick," Griffin replied. "When one of us has friends come in, the other one covers the register."

I snuck a peek at Audre, knowing she was loving that Griffin had called us his friends. She was trying not to smile, but her deep dimples gave her away. I grinned too.

Griffin was the social butterfly of the Book Nook, chatting up everyone from hipster writers to paint-stained artists. And his NYU buddies—most of them crushworthy, floppy-haired types—would sometimes drop by for free coffee. It *was* kind of flattering to be included in that circle, and I felt a sudden rush of confidence. If Griffin considered me a friend, there was no harm in asking him a few questions about getting into college. Maybe he would put my mind at ease after the Ms. Bliss fiasco.

I cleared my throat and took off my glasses. "Griffin?" I began. "Did you, um, when you applied to NYU, did you do lots of—"

"Drugs?" Griffin cut me off, his hazel eyes twinkling. He lazily rubbed a hand across the front of his worn blue T-shirt. "Dude, I must have been smoking *something*, because NYU is so not the right school for me."

"It's not?" Audre set down her latte with a frown, most likely tortured by visions of Griffin transferring to another city.

Griffin sighed. "It's a dope place and all, but these New York winters bring me down. Back in Santa Monica, I'd hit the beach with my friends every afternoon. I know it's messed up, but sometimes I miss high school. You know?"

Audre and I glanced at each other in horrified disbelief.

"You. Are. Crazy," Audre pronounced, staring at Griffin as if he'd just sprouted another gorgeous head.

"Don't get us started on high school," I jumped in, forgetting my nervousness. "Especially *today*. They played these disgusting love songs like 'I Wanna Be With You' over the PA system during lunch and—"

"Our English teacher made us watch that lame *Romeo and Juliet* movie—not even the Claire-and-Leo one," Audre groaned, rolling her eyes. I nodded emphatically.

Audre and I have been finishing each other's sentences since we met in the Prospect Park playground at age four. Griffin watched us with a small smirk, clearly amused.

"Not like English class doesn't suck on regular days," I added, and pointed to the stack of shiny paperbacks on the table in front of us. "I mean, there are so many incredible books in the world, and we're stuck reading dull, creepy stuff like *Heart of Darkness*." English was a sore point for me; it's usually my favorite subject, but our junior-year teacher, Mr. Whitmore, was a white-bearded snooze who sucked all the juiciness out of literature and droned on endlessly about grammar.

Griffin chuckled and ran a hand through his blond hair. "Dude, I hate to break it to you, but you still get assigned boring reading in college." Then his face lit up and he leaned forward. "Though you know what some of my friends have been into lately? Book groups."

"Book groups?" I echoed, feeling a pin-prick of curiosity.

"As in, like, Oprah?" Audre asked dubiously.

"But more fun," Griffin replied. "Just some friends getting together over beers once a month to chill and talk about, like, *On the Road*. It's cool 'cause *you* get to pick the books, not some stodgy teacher."

Hmm. Book groups. I pictured Audre, Scott, and myself hanging out in Audre's bedroom, drinking ciders that her older brother Langston would buy for us and debating the new Louise Rennison novel. True, Audre and Scott don't love to read as much as I do, and we *were* all swamped with school and SAT prep. Plus, Audre had her baking class, while Scott juggled Art Club, Student Council, and a zillion other extracurriculars—

Wait. That was *it*! I almost spilled my latte as I sat bolt upright. *Start your own club,* Ms. Bliss had said. A book group would count as a real activity, wouldn't it? I'd need a teacher's permission to make it official, but any sane adult would okay a club that was all about reading. And talk about showing colleges commitment *and* initiative. Take that, Ms. Bliss!

"Who's Ms. Bliss?" Griffin asked.

Oh, God. My cheeks burned and I

quickly drank more of my latte, hoping to disappear inside the giant mug. Had I spoken those last words *out loud*? One snicker from Audre confirmed my fear.

"Our guidance counselor," she explained casually. Then she elbowed me in the ribs. "And, Nors, I know what you're thinking, and the answer is a resounding no."

"Good for you, Psychic Hotline," I snapped, annoyed that she was so quick to burst my bubble. "So what if I want to start a book group? You're saying you wouldn't join?" That *couldn't* happen; I suck at organizing anything, so I'd need both Audre's and Scott's support to get a club off the ground.

Audre crossed her arms over her chest in her favorite you-are-not-changing-my-mind pose. "It'd be like having more homework."

"Not if you read good stuff," Griffin pointed out. He eased up out of the chair and stretched his arms above his head, giving us a delicious glimpse of his bare olive stomach. "And hey, you could even hold your meetings here. I'd be happy to bring you guys drinks."

Aha! This time, without even looking at Audre, I knew her dimples were showing. If anything was going to convince my stubborn best friend to take part in the group, it would be the chance to see more of her crush.

"I gotta hit the register before my boss finds me," the object of Audre's affection announced. "Norah, keep me posted 'bout this book group gig. I don't have time to join, but a friend of mine might be interested." When he looked my way, he grinned. Then, without warning, he strolled right up to me, crouched low, and leaned in toward my face.

I froze, and then flushed all over. What was going on? Was Griffin going to kiss me? My very first kiss—here, in the Book Nook? Would Audre get mad? Thank God I'd taken off my glasses, but I wished I'd at least put some Burt's Beeswax balm on my lips—

"Foam," Griffin said, wiping my upper lip with his warm thumb. "A danger of latte-drinking." He winked, stood up, and shot Audre a quick salute. "Later, ladies."

We sat there in stunned silence for

several seconds. Finally, I managed to turn to Audre and say, "He so likes you."

"Whatever," Audre replied. "He's a flirt. With me. With you. With everybody." She picked up a copy of *Fast Food Nation* from the table and thumbed through it. "Of course, that doesn't mean I'd be opposed to him serving me drinks. . . ." She glanced at me, her light brown eyes dancing.

Still shaky from the fake-out kiss, I barely dared believe my good luck. "At the book group?" I whispered. "You mean you'll do it, Aud?" Quickly, I told her about my face-off with Ms. Bliss and how starting the group could be my last hope.

"If it'll help you with college stuff, I'm there," Audre said firmly when I was finished. She squeezed my arm. "Consider me your second in command. I can even provide the snacks." Then she grinned wickedly. "And maybe that friend Griffin mentioned can provide the extra eye candy."

My heart fluttered for an instant. *Would* one of Griffin's NYU friends really join? That *could* be a nice bonus. I hadn't considered that, in addition to scoring me points with Ms. Bliss, this new club might improve my love life.

But, no. Good books *and* cute boys all at once?

While I was still in high school?

Not possible.

Two

"Oh . . . my . . . God! Mom! Help me, Mom, *please!*"

When I walked into my brownstone, I heard my thirteen-year-old sister's hysterical screams from upstairs. A stranger might think she'd injured herself, but I knew not to worry. I shut the door and noticed a note posted to the back, scrawled in my mother's messy handwriting: Don't forget to lock me in the morning.

I should probably explain about my parents. They're completely brilliant, and completely insane. My dad is a physics professor at Columbia University, and my mom is a research biologist. They're forever misplacing things, forgetting to lock the door, and sometimes forgetting they have two daughters—who both suck at science.

My sister, Stacey, careened down the stairs, almost colliding with me. Her curly dark hair was pinned up to her head, and she wore her fluffy bathrobe and platform flip-flops.

"Norah! Where's Mom?" she gasped. Then she grabbed me by the shoulders. "Have *you* seen my new satin-trimmed Aqua tank? Did you steal it?"

"Yeah, Stace." I shrugged out of her grasp. "All this time, I've been waiting for a chance to snatch your new top. Now I have it in my evil clutches and I'm never giving it back. Heh, heh, heh. " I rolled my eyes.

"Shut UP, Norah. Mom! MOM!" Stacey tore toward the kitchen just as our mother emerged carrying a pasta strainer and a pair of galoshes, as if the two items actually went together.

"Stacey Bloom, your shrieking is liable to puncture somebody's eardrums," Mom said. Then she pushed her enormous glasses up to her forehead and glanced at me. "Oh, Norah. Have you been here all this time?"

"I guess," I said, gazing around our living room. Sometimes I can't believe I live here. The only books on the shelves are science encyclopedias and medical journals. A photograph of Einstein sits above the fireplace. There are no novels or paintings in sight. If we Blooms didn't all look alike, I'd swear Stacey and I were adopted—from different families, of course.

I know I shouldn't complain. Scott's parents are divorced, and, even though that gives him a lot of freedom, he says it kind of sucks that they're never around.

But sometimes I think if would be okay if my family was a little less . . . around.

"What's the big deal about this top, anyway?" I asked Stacey.

She turned on me, and I noticed that her face was perfectly made up—raspberry lip gloss, sparkly blue eyeshadow, rosy blusher. Typical. I barely know how to use a mascara wand, and my baby sister is a mini makeup maven.

"I'm going to the movies with Dylan. In, like, ten minutes. He hasn't seen me in this tank yet. Plus, I *need* to wear pink because it's Valentine's Day—"

"Don't remind me," I said wearily.

"You don't have a date?" Stacey narrowed her big brown eyes at me and said what Ms. Bliss must have been thinking: "Ew, Norah, you are *so* pathetic."

Before I could reach for her throat, my dad stumbled out of the kitchen, trying to tamp down his mane of silver hair. Audre calls my dad's hair "The Thing." It really does have a life of its own. And it's really embarrassing.

"Hi, dear," Dad said to me. "Did you have fun at the movies?"

"*I'm* the one going to the movies, Daddy," Stacey cried, shoving past me. "And I can't find my new satin-trimmed tank top!"

"Oh," Dad said, raising his bushy eyebrows. "Was it pink?"

"Yes . . . ," Stacey said, drawing a deep breath so she could prepare for a really good scream. Seeing what was coming, I started for the staircase.

"Gosh, Stace. I'm sorry," Dad said. "I saw it in the laundry basket the other day so I lent it to my friend Hal, you know, the chemist? He needed to burn some material for an experiment—"

"BURN?" Stacey wailed.

"There's no need to make such a fuss about the spaghetti sauce," Mom said, coming back from whatever planet she'd been on.

I took the stairs two at a time, sprinted into my room, and locked the door behind me.

Ahh.

My room is a little rectangle of heaven. The wall above my bed is covered in black-and-white photos I've taken of Audre and Scott, colorful spreads I've clipped from *Time Out New York*, and an abstract blue painting that Tuesday Levine, a friend from my *Blank Canvas* days, made me for my birthday. The wall across from my bed has built-in shelves that are stuffed with novels, kind of like my own mini Book Nook.

I unzipped my hoodie, flung it on my blue velour armchair, and skimmed my shelves. It's a ritual: The first thing I do when I get home is read. Earlier, I'd been craving *Weetzie Bat*, but, after my hectic afternoon, I wanted something fluffier.

Speak? Too depressing. *Sense and Sensibility?* Too old-fashioned.

The choice was clear: I'd have to turn to my hidden stash.

I knelt down and looked under my bed. There they were. In a pile. Waiting for me.

Here's a secret: I love trashy paperback romances. Please don't mock me until you hear me out.

Yes, they're completely cheesy and have embarrassing titles like *Ravaged by Love* and *A Pirate's Passion*. The covers alone make me blush: women spilling out of their gowns, bare-chested guys with flowing hair, candles, canopy beds, ruffles. *So* not me. Of course, I hadn't told a soul—except for Audre—about my habit; it would kind of ruin my reputation as Literary Girl among my friends.

Not to mention my whole I-hate-romance stance.

But when I'm alone in my room, I love to indulge. The sweet, simple story lines are just yummy and comforting—like eating pistachio ice cream in a hot, bubbly bath. And, yeah, the sex scenes aren't bad either. Jane Austen is awesome, but nobody ever gets it on in *her* books. I tried to tell myself that when—or *if*—I finally got a boyfriend, I'd magically get over my secret addiction.

Until then, there was really no point in resisting.

I reached under my bed and pulled out an old reliable: *Dangerous Embraces*, by my favorite romance author, Irene O'Dell. She is—according to the photo inside the book—a glamorous old lady dripping in diamonds and wrapped in fur. I don't know how Irene does it, but she comes out with a brilliant new book every two months. *Dangerous Embraces* was a tale of forbidden desire between a milkmaid named Elsabetha and a count named Antonio. I sat cross-legged on my shag rug and was devouring the first line— *Elsabetha, a striking green-eyed beauty, had never known true love*—when my cell phone rang. It was Scott.

"Hey, gorgeous," he said, around a mouthful of what had to be Veggie Booty—he lives on the stuff.

"Ha," I snorted in response, glancing across my room to the full-length mirror. Explain to me how gangly limbs, fair skin, nearly-black eyes, and even darker hair add up to gorgeous. But ever since I met Scott in freshman-year algebra, he's acted as my professional confidence booster. It's probably because he has so much self-esteem, he feels the need to spread some of it around. He's always telling me and Audre that he doesn't understand how such sexy mamas as ourselves could possibly be single.

Really, it's too bad that he's gay.

"Are you holding up okay?" I asked him, leaning against my bed and peeking into *Dangerous Embraces*.

Scott's boyfriend, Chad (whom Audre and I secretly nicknamed "Cheekbones" because, honestly, those were his only good features) cruelly dumped him one week before V-Day, after they'd been together for six months. Instead of slumping into suicidal depression, as I surely would have, Scott threw himself into more activities, like volunteering to organize the upcoming Spring Formal. That morning, catching me and Audre in the hall before class, he'd declared that he was officially "taking a break from love." Scott has used this expression before, and his "break" usually lasts no more than, oh, two days. But this time, he seemed serious. I'd told him I fully supported the plan, since I was taking a break myself—a sixteen-year-long one.

"Naturally," Scott replied, chomping away. "As long as I have you and Audre, events to plan, a steady supply of Veggie Booty, and copious amounts of alcohol, I'm golden." He paused. "I was kidding about the alcohol part."

I giggled. "God, I wish you lived in Brooklyn." Like most Manhattanites, Scott rarely treks over to Park Slope; he sees all the outer boroughs as odd foreign lands— which Audre and I think is hilarious.

"Speaking of Brooklyn!" Scott exclaimed. "I hear it's going to be the setting for a certain fabulous *book group*."

"Why am I not surprised you know this?" I brushed a piece of lint off my black CBGB T-shirt. Scott is involved in every club known to man, so he gets the dirt on people before they've even *done* anything gossip-worthy. Still, despite Scott's popularity, he shuns the Plums of Millay and prefers to hang with Audre, me, and our cluster of low-key, artsy friends. I knew he'd be into the idea of a book group.

In fact, Scott told me, not only was *he* into the book group—which he'd heard about from Audre earlier that evening— but he'd already gotten Tuesday Levine and another friend of ours, Olivia Ramirez, to sign up. He'd created fifteen flyers, posted the news on Friendster, and drafted a permission statement for Mr. Whitmore to sign in the morning.

This is why I love Scott: He's crazy, but he gets things done. I was totally relieved that he'd taken care of all the messy details, and told him so.

"Oh, and I hope you don't mind," he added breezily. "I decided on a date: February twenty-fourth. Cool?"

"Uh, not so cool," I said, my stomach tightening. Suddenly, the whole thing felt all too real. "Scott, that's ten days away! I still need to—"

"What?" he challenged. "Everything's set."

I glanced down at *Dangerous Embraces*. "Well, we have to pick the books. . . ." I trailed off, wondering, for one nutty moment, if the group could start off by reading some classic Irene O'Dell.

"Chill, baby," Scott laughed. "*That* stresses you? You're like a walking library. Just don't assign us anything *too* smarty-pants, okay? I bet you're in the middle of *War and Peace* right now. Or the collected works of James Joyce?"

I snapped *Dangerous Embraces* shut, feeling a stab of shame. "Close," I lied. I *had* to keep my passion for paperback romances separate from my book group. This was, after all, an actual, serious, after-school club. My very own. And I couldn't allow anything to ruin what could be the most important undertaking of my life.

Well, next to convincing my mom to let me buy that green army jacket I'd been eyeing on eBay.

"Does this look decent up there?" I asked Audre the next afternoon, pinning the final thumbtack into Scott's flyer, and taking a step back. Scott had handed us a bunch of flyers at school that morning, and Audre and I had gone straight to the Book Nook that afternoon.

Now we studied the flyer's bright yellow

color and bold, block letters, which stood out against the cluttered bulletin board:

SEARCHING FOR SMART NEW FRIENDS . . .
AND SOME JUICY READS?
JOIN NORAH BLOOM'S BROOKLYN BOOK GROUP!
THE BOOK NOOK, PARK SLOPE,
SUNDAY, FEBRUARY 24, 12 P.M.
BRING JUST YOURSELF, YOUR IDEAS,
AND LOTS OF ENTHUSIASM!

"Better than decent," Griffin said, swinging by and playfully tugging Audre's pouffy ponytail. "I'm impressed."

"Our friend Scott did them," Audre said, beaming at her love. "You'll get to meet him next Sunday."

"Thanks for the reminder," Griffin said, grabbing an extra flyer from the stack at my feet. "I need to tell *my* friend about this."

"Right," Audre said, and shot me an impish grin. When Griffin had walked off, she sidled up to me and murmured, "Watch out, Nors. Between Griffin and his hot friend, we're *so* getting ourselves some Book Nook nookie."

I tried to grin back, but my stomach

was in knots. My minor freak-out on the phone last night was slowly mushrooming into a full-on panic attack. What if Griffin's hot friend brought still another friend? What if, like, five hundred total *strangers* showed up, all wanting to read different books? I'm not exactly good at meeting new people. I had a nightmarish vision of random teen, adult, and elderly readers gathered around a table at the Book Nook, their faces all turned eagerly toward me. What had I gotten myself into?

"Get a grip," Audre whispered, grabbing my elbow. I realized I'd been reaching up to remove the flyer from the board.

"Sorry," I whispered back. "I was just thinking, you know, that maybe this was a mistake."

"Forget it," Audre said, steering me away from the flyers. "It's too late now. Griffin knows about it, and, thanks to Scott, so does half of Millay."

Audre was right. The book group had been set into motion. There was nothing I could do but wait for that fateful Sunday to arrive.

Three

At noon on Sunday, February twenty-fourth, I walked into the Book Nook with just myself, my ideas, and lots of jangling nerves.

I'd meant to arrive earlier, but the morning had been hectic. I'd spent an hour choosing an outfit, finally settling on shredded jeans, my Belle & Sebastian T-shirt, a fuzzy blue cardigan, chandelier earrings, and blue Pumas. Next, I pulled out my cloth-bound journal and jotted down ideas for different books the group could discuss, like *Life of Pi* and *The Lovely Bones*. My first choice was *The Curious Incident of the Dog in the Night-Time*, which I'd seen on the shelf at the Book Nook—it had a cool orange paperback cover and a potentially good mystery story about an autistic kid. Still, I wasn't sure if the others in the group would go for it.

I was finishing off my book list when Tuesday Levine called. Her rich ex-boyfriend had flown her to his parents' house in Cabo San Lucas for the weekend to win her back, and now that they were together again, she was planning to spend all her free time glued to his side. I made a gagging motion at my mirror as I listened to my friend apologize for having to drop out of the book group. Tuesday has that kind of nauseating love karma, so I wasn't too surprised. But I also couldn't help wondering if her pulling out was a bad omen.

What if *no one* showed up?

Fortunately, at least Audre and Scott were there when I arrived, sitting at a big round table in the sun-bright café. Audre, fussing over a plate of her walnut-and-cranberry scones, was wearing a glittery headband and a sixties-style black-and-white checked dress with white boots. Scott, chatting on his cell, had on his usual uniform of a button-down short-sleeved shirt, slouchy slacks, and multiple wristbands. I was so grateful to see them that I almost burst into tears.

"I have bad news," Scott said before I could even sit down. He shut his phone and pushed a hand through his light brown curls. "Olivia Ramirez has mono, so she's gonna be out of school for, like, two months. Oh, and obviously she can't join the book group."

"And," Audre added carefully, watching me as if I might pass out any second, "Ha-Jin and Stephanie can't make it either. They're too stressed out by yearbook deadlines." She went back to arranging her scones, looking apologetic on behalf of all our friends.

"Then I was right!" I cried, plopping down in an empty seat.

"What, you mean Lindsay Lohan *is* Satan?" Scott asked, reaching across me for a scone. Audre slapped his hand away.

"No." I sighed. "I just had a sense of, like, *doom* this morning. If Tuesday and the other girls can't come, who does that leave us with?"

Just then, the front door swung open, letting in a blast of icy wind, followed by a tall girl decked out in a pink peacoat, Seven jeans, and spike-heeled black boots. She paused with her hand on her slim hip, as if she were posing, then whipped off her wraparound shades and shook out her chin-length raven hair. One of the store cats—Agatha Christie, I think—crept up to the girl and purred, and she jerked away, shuddering in disgust.

"Plum alert," Audre whispered, nudging me.

I nodded. There was no way a girl like *that* would be here for our book group. But when Griffin came out from behind the register and wrapped his arms around the Plum type, I gasped and Audre immediately grabbed my hand.

"What's wrong?" Scott asked, glancing up; he'd been text-messaging under the table.

"Everything," I answered softly, watching in disbelief as Griffin kissed the girl on each cheek.

"You made it!" I heard him exclaim. "They're in the back."

Slowly, Audre turned her head to gaze at me, horrified.

"*That's* the friend?" she whispered.

"What about the—the sexy guy?" I stammered.

"What sexy guy?" Scott demanded,

poking my arm. "You mean him?" He pointed at Griffin just as he was approaching our table, one hand on the glam girl's elbow.

"Don't *point*," Audre hissed, her cheeks going crimson. "That's the boy I have a crush on, remember?"

Scott had heard me and Audre gossip aplenty about Griffin in school, but he hadn't yet seen the Book Nook hottie in the flesh. "Oops," Scott said, ducking his head as Griffin arrived at our table.

"Guys, this is my friend, Francesca Cantone," Griffin said, all grins as he motioned to the princess at his side. "She's supersmart, and a big reader, so watch out."

"Oh, Griffy. I am so *not* a big reader!" Francesca giggled, and swatted Griffin's ripped upper arm. Something about her reaction seemed forced, as if she were acting out the role of Ditzy Girl on a WB sitcom. I hated her already. Up close, she was even more perfect—tan skin, carefully plucked eyebrows, pouty lips. And, I couldn't help but notice as she sat down and took off her peacoat, actual cleavage enhanced by a tight black V-neck sweater. She barely glanced at the rest of us and instantly started examining herself in her Stila compact.

Now the question was, when Griffin said "friend," did he actually mean "friend with benefits"?

Audre, who must have been wondering the same thing, tightened her kung fu grip on my hand and glared at Francesca with a murderous glint in her eyes.

Griffin, as always, was happily oblivious. "You must be the famous Scott," he was saying, leaning across the table to shake Scott's hand. "Dude, nice flyers."

"I bet you say that to all the boys," Scott replied, his green eyes sparkling.

I kicked him under the table. Even when he's taking a break from love, Scott sometimes hits on straight guys, just to see them blush.

But the ever-chill Griffin only laughed. "Why don't y'all settle in and I'll make some coffee?" he asked.

"Skim latte for me, sweetie," Francesca called loudly as Griffin ambled off.

"You're on a diet, huh?" Audre spoke up, glaring at Francesca. Audre thinks diets are ridiculous. I guess most future pastry chefs do.

For a minute, Francesca looked surprised, but then she seemed to collect herself, rotated a diamond stud in her left ear, and slowly sized Audre up. "What's it to *you*?" she snapped.

"Oh, crap," Scott and I muttered at the same time. Getting bitchy on Audre is never a good idea.

"Well, I'm the vice president of this book group," Audre retorted, inventing the position for herself on the spot. "And I'm also a friend of Griffin's. How do *you* even know him? Are you also at NYU?"

Scott and I turned our heads from one girl to the next, as if we were watching a Ping-Pong match.

"No. I'm a senior in high school," Francesca answered shortly.

Oh. I glanced at Audre, knowing she was absorbing this news with interest. Francesca's being in the group still seemed random, but her being in high school at least made more sense. Now that I thought about it, Griffin probably wouldn't have recommended a high school book group to his *college* friends—let alone a hot boy. Audre and I had just been stuck in the land of wishful thinking.

"So where did you meet Griffin?" Audre pressed on, not even attempting to be subtle.

"We met at an exhibit at the Guggenheim this past fall," Francesca replied snidely. "But you're from Brooklyn, so you wouldn't even know what that is, right? *I* live in Manhattan—"

"You do?" Scott jumped in, clearly trying to play peacemaker. "Where do you go to school?"

Francesca's face turned stony, and a flicker of something I couldn't quite read flashed in her gray eyes. "Uptown," she replied icily. End of discussion.

"For your information, I know exactly what the Guggenheim is," Audre snapped, still staring Francesca down. "What, you think you're *better* than people from Brooklyn?"

Yikes. Scott and I exchanged a worried glance. But before a full-on catfight could explode, an unfamiliar male voice spoke directly behind me:

"Uh, is this the sci-fi group?"

Almost afraid to look, I turned around to find two boys I'd never seen before. They both seemed to be about sixteen. The one who'd spoken shrugged at me; he was Indian-American, with wavy brown hair, wire-frame glasses, and a hooded sweatshirt that said *Hart Crane Weather Club*. Hart Crane is this high school in Park Slope, where Audre and I almost went before our parents decided on Millay. *And the boys there,* I decided in that moment, *are not any better than what Millay has to offer.* The other boy was a few inches taller, and thin; he had messy dark hair and wore jeans and a plaid button-down shirt, the sleeves crookedly rolled up. He was staring at the floor.

"Sci-fi group?" I repeated. What the hell? I glanced around the café to see if any people wearing Star Trek costumes had gathered, but besides us, there was only a young mom with her baby, and a couple doing a crossword puzzle.

"Noon? The twenty-fourth? At the Book Nook?" Weather Club boy asked, reaching into his bookbag. "I got this flyer—"

Francesca cut him off with a loud jangle of her Tiffany charm bracelet. "Whatever. You can join us if you *want*." She rolled her eyes, as if she were doing the world a huge favor by being nice to a dork.

Weather Club boy shrugged, then gamely plunked down at the table. "I'm Neil Singh," he announced, and then gestured to his silent friend, who was taking the seat beside him. "And that's my buddy James Roth."

I gazed in wonder at the new arrivals. How had *this* little ragtag group come together?

Audre and Francesca were busy baring their teeth, and Griffin had returned to serve the coffee, so Scott hurriedly did the introductions, making sure to call me "our fearless leader"—which made me want to kick him again.

"Haven't we met before?" Neil asked Francesca, and I cringed. Had Weather Club boy really just used the most predictable line in pick-up history? Francesca didn't respond; she just twisted the faux-emerald ring on her finger. I glanced at James to see if he, too, was drooling over Francesca, but he was bent over, his hair in his eyes, scribbling something on a napkin.

Um, freak?

"Okay!" I said, trying to get it together. If this bizarre mix of kids *was* the book group, then I had to make us work somehow. Otherwise, I might as well go crawling back into Ms. Bliss's perfumed office with a giant FAILURE sign attached to my forehead. My hands were trembling a little, so I covered them with my cloth-bound journal, hoping no one would notice. "What books would people like to read?" I asked, chewing my bottom lip.

After a minute of heart-pounding silence, Neil cleared this throat.

"*I, Robot*," he said flatly. When nobody responded, he added, "I guess I'd settle for *Eragon*, but it's kinda over by now, huh?"

"Well," I replied shakily, thinking I'd rather go through Chinese water torture than read *Eragon* for fun.

James looked up from his napkin, directly at me. "This *isn't* a sci-fi book club, is it?" he asked, and there seemed to be relief in his voice. He had blue eyes, I noticed. Light blue. I shook my head in response, and he promptly returned to his mysterious scribbles.

"*Kitchen Confidential*?" Audre suggested, in between shooting death looks at Francesca.

"Uh . . ." Francesca herself had her chin in her hands and seemed to be deep in concentration, as if wrestling with a deep philosophical problem. Finally, she straightened up, and looking hopeful, said, "*Gossip Girl*?"

"*Boy Meets Boy*?" Scott offered, fiddling with his wristbands.

All the suggestions were good, but the problem was, I'd read all those books. I wanted something new. I opened my cloth-bound book and glanced at my first choice. There was no harm in suggesting it, right?

I coughed into my fist. "What about—"

"*The Curious Incident of the Dog in the Night-Time*?" James spoke, stealing the words off my tongue.

I glanced up at him, startled, and he laughed. His smile was crooked, I thought, in an almost-charming way. With his slim build and dark hair, he looked kind of like the lead singer of Maroon 5. Only not hot.

"Sorry," he said. "Was that what you—?"

"Um, yeah, I guess," I shut my note-book, weirded out by the coincidence.

"I think two people agreeing is the best we're gonna get," Audre declared "*Curious

Whatever-Whatever it is." She lifted up her plate of pastries. "Now, who wants scones?"

Everybody did, even Francesca. It seemed we were *all* mildly freaked by the randomness of the group. And sugar is always helpful in times of crisis.

"Okay, how much did that suck?" I asked Audre fifteen minutes later as we huddled on a bench in Prospect Park for postmeeting gossip.

After exchanging e-mail addresses and phone numbers, the group had scattered; Scott returned to Manhattan for an art class, Neil and James disappeared to God knows where, and Francesca—to Audre's chagrin—stayed to chat with Griffin, who'd urged us all to return to the Book Nook for our next session, in March.

If there ever *was* a next session. I was surprised we'd made it through the first.

"Do you think she's prettier than me?" was Audre's response. She was chewing her fingernails, looking—for possibly the first time in her life—insecure.

"Francesca? Give me a break." I rolled my eyes. "Besides, there's something . . . *off* about her, don't you think?" I thought back to how she hadn't told us where she went to school. "Like she's *hiding* something."

Audre shook her head. "Nors, you're paranoid. You always think people are hiding things."

"That's because, most of the time, they are."

Audre wrapped her hand-knit yellow scarf around her neck. "All she's hiding is the fact she and Griffin are hooking up." Her mouth turned down at the corners. "Nors, should we throw in the towel and join a convent?"

"The world's first Jewish nun," I mused, staring into space. "I could be famous!"

Audre snorted, and I gave her a light shove.

"Anyway, what are you complaining about?" I added. "At least you've been kissed, dork."

She groaned. "Derek Dawson does not count." Freshman year, Audre sort of dated this skinny soccer player with curly hair and braces, but she dumped him when he didn't know what brioche was. (And people think

I'm picky). Derek has filled out, lost the braces, and in my opinion gotten pretty good-looking—and I'm positive he still likes Audre. I'm always telling her to give him another chance. Or at least another kiss.

Fact: Being sixteen and kissless is beyond depressing. I obsessed over it constantly. On the one hand, kissing seemed so easy: a boy's lips against yours. But then, it seemed scary and impossible. How did you figure out the angle at which to tilt your head, or where your nose went? And how did you even *get* to that point, when you were close enough to a boy to see the shape of his mouth, and feel his warm breath, and be sure that he was going to lean in and . . . *do* it?

"What did you think of Neil and James, those Hart Crane guys?" Audre was asking as we got up off the bench and headed for home. "Lame, huh?"

My mind jumped from kisses to the boys in question. *What would it be like to kiss James?* I wondered, then shook my head. Where had *that* thought come from? My cheeks got very hot for a second, then went back to normal.

"Lame," I agreed. "Totally lame."

Four

Speaking of *lame*, picture this:

Saturday night, the first weekend in March. I, Norah Bloom, am sitting in a packed, very happening Park Slope bar called Art House. It's the only bar in the neighborhood that doesn't card, so tons of high school kids are there, cramming into the striped booths, flirting in front of the kitschy movie posters, and sitting on the polka-dot bar stools. The music—old-school hip-hop, which I love—is thumping, and tons of people, including some of my closest friends, are getting down on the circular dance floor. But I am tucked away in a corner booth . . . reading.

Yes, reading.

Let me backtrack. Audre's awesome big brother, Langston—awesome because he buys us beer *and* has long dreads, a sparkling smile, and tons of hotness to spare—was on spring break from Yale and throwing a "Come As You Aren't" birthday party at Art House.

Langston's costume birthday bashes at Art House—which he's been doing every year since high school—are practically legendary, so even Scott travels to Brooklyn for them. Last year's theme was "Bonnie & Clyde," and when Scott showed up in his gangster outfit, he got three guys' numbers. (Audre and I came as flappers, but all we got were skeezy stares from freshman boys at the bar.)

This year, Scott had dressed as a football jock, complete with shoulder pads and a helmet. And Audre had come dressed as a good girl—pigtails, white button-down shirt, plaid skirt, knee socks, the works. This costume was sort of silly because, as Scott and I had pointed out, Audre *is* a good girl. But, like most people, I guess Aud prefers to imagine she's naughtier than she actually is.

As for me, I'd come—with Stacey's help—as a Plum. My sister had cajoled me into a cashmere white halter dress and pointy-toed sling-backs. My hair fell loose around my shoulders, my eyes were smudged with liner, and my lips were glossy. The outfit had seemed funny at home, but the instant I'd entered the bar on Scott's arm, I'd felt naked and completely uncomfortable. Wearing a backless dress while pressing up against a million sweaty, dancing bodies is not a good plan. And no matter how firmly Scott insisted that I looked "hot," I suddenly wanted nothing more than to hide away forever.

I'm not a big party person.

Thank God I'd come prepared: In my beaded bag was a copy of *The Curious Incident of the Dog in the Night-Time*, which I was loving. So, as soon as Audre and Scott took their virgin martinis to the dance floor, I made my escape. *It's not as bad as actually* leaving *Art House,* I told myself as I settled down with the book. Still, I knew if Audre found me she'd strangle me for being so antisocial. But when I leaned over the flickering tea lights and started reading,

I forgot about Audre and everyone else. I was turning to the last page when—

"Can I steal your light?"

"Huh?" Blinking, I lifted my head and saw a boy sitting in the booth across from me, half-reaching for the candle.

"Norah?" he asked, looking even more surprised than I felt.

He *knew* me? Still out of it, I took in the boy's rumpled shirt, blue eyes, and tousled dark hair. *Hello!* It was James, from the book group.

But what was he doing *here*?

Then I noticed he was holding a pen, and on the table in front of him was a napkin he'd clearly been writing on. Again. I squinted, trying to make out the words.

"Are you . . . writing *poetry*?" I asked, my voice disdainful. "At a *bar*?" *What a weirdo,* I almost added.

James stared at me blankly, and then his face broke into a slow smile. "Are you . . . reading?" he shot back. "At a *bar*?"

Oh, God. My cheeks flamed. He had a point.

We were *both* weirdos.

I started giggling. "Sorry. Pot, kettle, black, right?"

He nodded. "Isn't that a Wilco song?"

I grinned. "They're one of my favorite bands." Our eyes met for an instant, and I felt a weird, almost electric *zing* of energy.

I didn't think James felt anything, though, because he glanced away and cleared his throat. "I'm sorry I interrupted you. I, um, I didn't recognize you at first."

Right. My skimpy halter dress. I felt a rush of embarrassment and tried as hard as I could not to wrap my arms around my seminude self.

"Oh," I blurted. "Yeah. This isn't, like, *me.*"

Great, Norah. Way to make sense there.

But when I saw James's mouth turn up in a crooked grin, I realized he got what I meant. Sort of. Relaxing a bit, I explained about Langston's "Come As You Aren't" bash, and James confessed that he'd also escaped—from a crappy game of pool at the other end of the bar.

After he'd pointed out said pool game—which Neil from the book group and a group of other boys were playing—James then gestured to the book in my hand. "I just finished," he said. "What do you think?"

"It kicks ass, doesn't it?" I asked excitedly, and James nodded, his face lighting up.

And then we jumped into the best conversation I'd ever had in my life.

We talked about different novels and poems—stuff we'd loved, or hated. We both agreed that Virginia Euwer Wolff was phenomenal, but James preferred *True Believer*, while I liked *Make Lemonade*. We quoted e.e. cummings to each other, and laughed when we messed up on the same lines ("the voice of your eyes is deeper than all roses . . ."). And it felt—I know it's dorky, so I apologize in advance—like our own private book group. *This is me,* I thought, forgetting my outfit and makeup, and feeling happily flushed. I hadn't imagined I could ever talk about books like this with a *boy*. Most guys I knew at Millay didn't read much, except maybe for graphic novels. James was different.

"I'll read basically anything," he said with a shrug, smiling shyly.

But probably not trashy romances.

Suddenly I pictured him bent over an Irene O'Dell paperback, his dark hair in his eyes, and I bit back a laugh. Then I wondered if his room looked like mine—heaps of books everywhere—but thinking about James's bedroom made me blush, in a very junior high way. To get my mind off the James-plus-bed equation, I asked him if he liked the poet Philippa Askance.

"She's amazing," James replied. "And not just 'cause she's cute." Now *he* blushed, ducking his head.

My heart was suddenly knocking hard against my ribs, as if it were trying to get my attention. Was it because I wanted James to say . . . *I* was cute?

"Cutie! Where were you all this time?"

I glanced up in a daze to see Scott standing at my elbow, holding his football helmet. The dance floor behind him was almost empty, and Audre and Langston were putting on their coats. How long had James and I been talking? I hadn't even remembered to get nervous, like I usually do around boys. And the strange thing was, I didn't *want* us to stop talking. I bit my lip, trying to think of a polite way to ask Scott to disappear.

But then James was getting to his feet, napkin poem in hand. My stomach sank. That was it? Maybe he hadn't thought our conversation was all that incredible. I sized him up. Now that James was standing, I saw how tall he was, and how his shoulders, under his dark blue T-shirt, were broad. I felt a tingling along my limbs.

The first time I'd seen him, I hadn't thought James was hot.

Clearly, I'd been insane.

He glanced at me and Scott and gave us a short nod, in that typical boy way—it's like they can't speak the words "hi" or "bye" so they just *nod*. I hate it.

But before James turned to go, he said, "See you at the next meeting, Norah?"

The sound of my name in his voice— which was surprisingly deep—made my heart skip a couple of beats. I'd never paid so much attention to my heart before.

I managed to nod, he loped off, and Scott plunked down into his empty seat.

"Love connection?" he teased, grinning.

I shrugged, feeling shaky. "Nah. We just chatted," I covered, not really wanting to explain my spinning feelings. I didn't know *what* had happened between me and James. But I did know that I couldn't wait for the next meeting of the book group.

Five

"I hated it," Francesca announced the minute our meeting began. She threw her copy of *The Curious Incident of the Dog in the Night-Time* on the Book Nook's table and shuddered, like the book was contagious. "The worst thing I've ever read." Then she reached into her tiny metallic clutch to pull out a tube of lip gloss.

Fiddling with the round buttons on my vintage blouse, I peeked into my cloth-bound journal. Last night, I'd brainstormed a bunch of discussion questions like "Who was your favorite character?" and "What do you think the ending meant?" Now the questions seemed loser-ish.

"Did *anybody* like it?" I asked, looking at the faces around me.

Audre was taking her homemade chocolate bark out of a Baggie so she could avoid my eyes. She'd already told me the night before that she thought the book was bizarre.

Scott smiled sheepishly behind his bag of Veggie booty and whispered, "I didn't have time to finish it."

Neil was ignoring everyone and reading *The Fellowship of the Ring,* which said it all.

And James wasn't there.

Where is *he?* I wondered. I was dying to ask Neil but I didn't want to seem desperate. I glanced outside the windows at the raging late March rainstorm. Maybe James had been struck by lightning? Or, more likely, he'd just dropped out. Sure, he'd said *See you at the next meeting,* but that didn't mean anything. He'd probably decided I was a complete nerd after we'd talked at Art House. By now he'd joined a new, mind-blowing book group, led by a busty girl with shimmery blond hair who was as good at English as she was at kissing—

"Sorry I'm late."

My stomach jumped as I turned around.

James was standing at the table, hands in the pockets of his baggy khakis. I'd never been happier to see anyone in my life. He was soaking wet; his dark hair was plastered to his head and his lashes—long for a boy's—were damp with droplets of water. When he sat down, he pulled his sweatshirt off over his head. He had on a plain white T-shirt underneath. When he caught me staring, he raised his eyebrows, and I looked away. He didn't at all acknowledge the fact that we'd met at Art House a couple of weeks before.

And suddenly I recognized the symptoms I'd had over the past two weeks: trembling knees, fluttery breath, flushed cheeks. I'd thought I was coming down with a cold. But no.

I had a crush on James.

A bad one.

When I get crushes they famously go *nowhere*—sometimes because I do something stupid to mess them up, but usually because the boy just isn't into me. My last crush was on Seamus Higgins, who edited *Blank Canvas*. He had a dark goatee and smelled like clove cigarettes and once in a while he'd smile at me. My hopes crashed and burned one afternoon when I walked in on him and Lydia Rivera, the copy editor, making out in the *Blank Canvas* office. Seamus had glanced up and snapped, "Could you leave, Nina?" I left and went home and wrote dumb things like "Love = Pain" in my cloth-bound journal and listened to the Yeah Yeah Yeahs and decided that I'd never fall for a stupid boy again. But crushes, like colds, usually sneak up on you when you least expect them.

"Ms. Bloom," Scott said in a British accent, popping a handful of Veggie Booty into his mouth. "Aren't you going to scold Sir James for being tardy?" Scott only whips out his fake accents when he wants to tease me; ever since Art House, his big joke was that James and I were secret lovers. I shot Scott a glare, but he was saved by his cell phone ringing. When he glanced at the number on the screen, he excused himself from the table.

Whew.

"I had to walk my little sister to her dance class," James explained, unfolding a copy of the *Onion* in his lap.

Terrific. On top of everything else, he had to be the perfect big brother. Couldn't he have said he'd been at rugby practice and totally turned me off?

"You're right on time," Francesca breathed, smiling at James. Was she *flirting* with him? Maybe she'd noticed his secret hotness too. But wasn't she more into Griffin? "I was just about to give my ideas for the next meeting," she added coyly.

Who asked you? I thought. We hadn't even discussed the first book yet. I felt it in the pit of my stomach: Things were going downhill, and fast.

Tossing her hair, Francesca unfolded a pink piece of paper and carefully read out loud: "*The A-List, The Au Pairs, Summer Boys, South Beach, Sloppy Firsts, The Devil Wears Prada*—"

"Whoa," I cut in, taken aback by her chick-lit bonanza. I thought I saw James glance at me and smile, but then he went back to reading the paper.

Francesca narrowed her eyes. "Are you making fun of me, Norah?"

"No, but you just listed like a million

books!" I replied, rolling my eyes. Paranoid much?

Audre, who was already in a pissy mood after seeing Griffin quickly kiss Francesca on the lips when she'd arrived that day, crossed her arms over her chest, her red plastic bracelets clinking together. "You mean you actually care what we read?" she asked Francesca.

Oh, boy. Here we went again.

Francesca's gray eyes blazed. "*Excuse me?*"

"How about *Do Androids Dream of Electric Sheep*?" Neil piped up, still clinging to his sci-fi dreams.

"I've read that already," Francesca said distractedly, clearly eager to get back to Audre. Then her cheeks turned pink and she glanced quickly at Neil. "Or *not*," she added snidely. "Why would I bother with some ridiculous book about *androids*?"

I studied Francesca, wondering why she'd snapped at Neil so abruptly.

But Audre didn't seem to notice; she was on a roll. "We all know why you *really* joined this group," she told Francesca.

Francesca's normally tan skin looked

paler than usual as she turned back to Audre. "What . . . are you . . . talking about?" she whispered.

"You joined for college, right?" I jumped in, hoping to stop Audre before she went off on a Griffin rant. "I mean, to put on your record? That's why I—"

"No," Francesca replied curtly. "I already got in early to Dartmouth."

Dartmouth? How? Had she slept with the admissions officer?

Then, for a crazy second, I wondered if Francesca had been sentenced to this book group by some vindictive guidance counselor. Maybe she'd gotten into trouble at school and this was her punishment—a kind of community-outreach to geeks.

"Please. The real reason is Griffin," Audre spat. "All you care about is getting your claws into—"

"I heard my name."

Griffin, forever the master of bad timing, appeared, carrying a bunch of steaming coffee mugs. He set them down and stole a piece of chocolate bark from Audre. "How are my favorite book lovers?" he asked with a wide smile.

All of a sudden I felt like crying. Griffin had been so sweet helping me start the group, and now the whole thing was going down the toilet. Nobody liked the first book. Scott was too busy. Francesca and Audre were going to strangle each other. Neil only lived for sci-fi. And James . . . James was weird and unpredictable, and my crush on him was only going to lead to disaster when he inevitably rejected me.

I made an executive decision.

"We're done," I announced, pushing my chair back. I thought of Ms. Bliss. *Good-bye, Vassar.* My voice wobbled a little, which made me feel even worse. "The book group is over. I'm calling it off."

Audre gasped and looked at me. "Nors, you didn't even consult me! And I'm the vice president."

"Uh, Aud, you made that up, remember?" I replied, rolling my eyes.

"Over?" Francesca cried, looking alarmed. What did she care?

James looked up from the *Onion*, biting his lower lip in this incredibly sexy way. "Are you serious?" he asked me anxiously, and I felt my stomach twist. What did *he* care?

Neil shrugged, propping *The Fellowship of the Ring* up against his coffee mug. "Fine by me," he declared.

Scott returned to the table then, wearing an apologetic smile. "Student Council crisis," he explained, snapping his phone shut. "What did I miss?" He looked around at everyone's miserable faces, and his grin slowly deflated.

"Dude, Norah ended the book group," Griffin told him, also, weirdly, looking miserable. Then, glancing at me, Griffin's face brightened. "Though, hey, maybe you'll change your mind when you hear my awesome news."

"What is it?" I asked Griffin numbly, guessing that he'd won some surfing contest.

"I just met Philippa Askance." Griffin grinned. "You know, the writer?"

I nodded, my pulse racing. Philippa Askance had been *here*? James and I had just talked about her at Art House! She's this an incredible writer—she's only nineteen, and her gritty novel in verse, *Bitter Ironies*, was a huge hit. But she's mainly cool because she's a mystery. Besides the author photo on the back of the book—bleached-blond hair in a spiky do, combat boots, a skirt held together by safety pins, and a delicate face hidden in the shadows—no one *had ever seen her*. She never gave readings or interviews and, according to a teen blog I'd read, Philippa was now working on her top-secret second novel and never left her house. So Griffin's news *was* superexciting. Even Audre, Francesca, and the others perked up; Philippa's that big of a celebrity.

"What did she say?" James asked, his blue eyes sparkling. I felt a flash of jealousy, kind of like I'd had at Art House when James had said Philippa was cute.

"Nothing, of course." Griffin shook his head. "She was browsing at the shelves and had these giant shades on, but I recognized her from her author photo, and was like, 'Dude, I'm a fan. Come give a reading at the Book Nook!' But then she bolted like I'd, I don't know, asked her to *sleep* with me or something."

Probably 90 percent of the book group blushed when he said that.

"So here was my idea," Griffin went on, leaning against the back of Francesca's chair.

"Why don't *you* guys try to get Philippa Askance to read at the Book Nook? She doesn't care about *me*, but maybe if it came from, like, a high school book group, she'd think that was really cool, and a good cause and all."

I sat up straighter, forgetting my unhappiness. Griffin was a genius! I would have chewed off my left arm to meet Philippa, and now here was my chance. How stupid would it be to cancel the book group when we could actually organize something this exciting?

To my shock, everyone else, except for Neil, seemed to be having the exact same reaction. They were all nodding and telling Griffin what a great idea this was. I didn't get it—I assumed all the others had wanted the group to just roll over and die.

But somehow we were back on track.

James, adorably energized, suggested we set up a separate meeting to map out a Philippa plan of attack: We knew she lived in Park Slope, so some of us could hunt around the neighborhood for her, while the others tried to get in touch with her agent or editor. We agreed to schedule our next

Philippa gathering for next Saturday.

Then, because the group's vibe was suddenly so mellow and almost, well, *friendly*, I decided not to ruin it by shooting down Francesca's earlier suggestions.

"Let's read *The Devil Wears Prada*," I picked randomly, "for our next real meeting, in April."

Neil, James, and Scott groaned, Francesca beamed at me like I was her new best friend, and Audre elbowed me in the ribs. It didn't matter. Nothing could bother me anymore. Philippa Askance would give a reading at the Book Nook, my club wasn't a total flop, and best of all, I was definitely going to see James again.

Six

"Don't kill me," Audre said over the phone as I walked briskly up Seventh Avenue, my cell tucked between my chin and my shoulder. "But I can't make it to Operation: Find Philippa. My baking class got rescheduled, and if I don't go, my parents will use that against me until the end of time."

It was a sun-soaked Saturday—the first day in March that felt like spring—and I was flip-flopping toward the Starbucks on Carroll Street where the book group was supposed to meet. (Over e-mail, we'd decided against the Book Nook because Griffin doesn't work there on Saturdays, and this didn't count as an "official" meeting.) In addition to my flip-flops, I was celebrating the weather with the cropped, olive-green eBay jacket my mom had finally lent me money for. That, paired with a tank top and jeans, was enough. I love when it starts to get warm out.

"I totally understand," I told Audre, even though her news was a bit of a bummer. Audre's parents, the usually-chill Mr. and Mrs. Legrand, think their Gourmet Diva daughter should aim for Yale, like Langston. But Audre is all about cooking school, so she and her 'rents clash. She takes this baking class at a community college to prove to them she's serious about it.

"So now you and Scott have *both* bailed," I added, heading toward Carroll Street. "He's hosting some charity auction for Millay today. Or maybe that was last week. I can't keep track."

"Well, say hi to James for me—if you can," Audre laughed. Of course I'd already filled my best friend in on my crush—it's impossible for me to keep secrets from Audre, even if I want to. She'd already guessed I was head over heels when, according to her, I'd been "checking out his fine, rain-drenched body at the last meeting." I hadn't denied it.

Then I saw James for real, standing outside Starbucks with his arms crossed over his chest, looking thoughtful and gorgeous.

"Gotta go," I whispered to Audre, clicking off.

"Um, hey, Norah. I think it's just you and me," I heard James say as I approached him, my pulse tapping like crazy.

"What do you mean?" I stopped short, so I wouldn't have to come too close. Sitting across from James in the darkness of Art House, practically half-naked, had somehow been comfortable; standing with him in a regular-me outfit in broad daylight was freaking me out. Normal, right?

"Neil has a math team competition this weekend," James explained, not really looking at me. "And Francesca showed up like a second ago, but when I told her I didn't think anyone else was coming, she made up some excuse and ran away."

Only because Griffin's not here, I thought, annoyed on Audre's behalf. Then I remembered Audre. And Scott.

James was right. It *was* just the two of us.

"So . . . ," I said, firmly telling myself

that we were not on a date, "how should we work this?"

James brushed his thick, dark hair out of his eyes. "Well, before Francesca left, she promised she'd try to call Philippa's agent on Monday. And Neil said he'd look up her editor." He shrugged. "I guess we could kind of walk around and see if we run into her somewhere?"

Semistalking Philippa actually sounded like fun, so before I could get too nervous, I agreed.

Silently, we wandered up and down side streets, under blooming trees, the sun warming us. Park Slope is laid out in a neat little grid, so it's easy to roam for a while and not get lost. We were turning the corner onto 3rd Street when we bumped into my next-door neighbor, this old lady, Mrs. Ferber.

I hate to use the term "nosy," but Mrs. Ferber begs for it; she's always looking out her window to see my family's comings and goings and is forever catching me and Stacey out by the trash cans, asking us when we plan on getting married. She also never seems to remember which sister is which.

True to form, Mrs. Ferber squinted up

at me from under the brim of her ridiculous hot pink sun hat, clearly trying to figure out who I was.

"The Bloom girl!" she cried at last, clapping her hands together in excitement as James looked obviously amused. Then, her silver curls trembling, she pointed to James. "*Another* boyfriend?" she cackled.

I felt my cheeks grow hot. Okay. She *definitely* thought I was Stacey. Just last week, Stacey had said that Mrs. Ferber had spied on her and Dylan when they were kissing good night on our stoop.

"Uh, no," I began, staring down and wishing the sidewalk beneath my feet had a trapdoor. "You're thinking of—"

"Well, he's *much* more handsome than the last one," Mrs. Ferber cut in. Then, patting me on the shoulder, she added an emphatic "Good for you!" before tottering off.

I stood there, my eyes shut, contemplating suicide.

When I dared peek at James, he was studying the ground, his ears very red. He glanced at me and gave his sideways grin.

"You must run into people in the neighborhood a lot," he finally spoke, swallowing down what sounded suspiciously like a laugh. "I mean, I know I do."

It was a relief to break the silence—and avoid talking about what Mrs. Ferber had said. "Yeah, I'm used to it. I've lived here all my life. Have you?" I asked as we started walking again.

James nodded. "But it's weird, because as well as I think I know the Slope, I'm always discovering new stuff—like that." He pointed across the street to a light blue limestone house.

"What about it?" I asked. We stopped walking and both stared across the street.

"It's the only blue house on the whole street," James replied, as if this were obvious. "When you really notice it is at night, because it glows, like a ghost."

I looked at the house, and then turned to look at James, examining his profile. *He's so smart,* I thought, my heart beating faster. The way he saw the world made me realize that he must have been a good poet—better than anyone on *Blank Canvas,* in any case. I wished I had the nerve to ask to read his poetry.

James was still looking at the house across the street, so he backed up and sat on one of the brownstone stoops. Without thinking, I sat beside him, hugging my knees, still studying the side of his face.

"It's beautiful," I finally whispered, meaning the house. Kind of.

James turned to me, his blue eyes serious. "And you," he said.

My breath caught. *What?*

"You're like that house," James went on. "You've always been in this neighborhood, but I'd never even seen you before the book group."

"Oh. Right." *Hello, moron! Of course he didn't mean you're beautiful.*

We fell silent again, and I noticed that we were sitting very close together on the stoop. The sun was right overhead, so I slipped off my jacket and draped it across my lap. As I was doing that, my arm brushed James's, and I felt the warmth of his skin. He smelled clean and sweet, like vanilla. Suddenly, I was shaking. I wanted to touch James for real, on purpose, to run my fingers through his hair.

As if James knew what I was thinking,

he turned his head and held my gaze. His eyes looked darker than usual, and he swallowed hard.

"Norah?" he said quietly.

"Yeah?" I asked.

"Um," he replied. And then he leaned in toward me.

You know when something absolutely insane and wonderful is happening and time sort of slows down? James was coming closer, and his lips were inches from mine, and very slowly I was realizing, *He . . . is . . . going . . . to . . . kiss . . . me.* This was *it*: that delicious prekiss moment I'd wondered about for so long! My heart hammering, I leaned in to meet him halfway and—

The door of the brownstone behind us creaked open loudly, and someone stepped out onto the stoop. A dog barked.

James pulled back immediately, and I spun around to see the evil person who had interrupted what was going to be my amazing, unforgettable first kiss.

It was Philippa Askance.

Her spiky, bleached-blond hair was pulled up in a high ponytail and, behind oversized shades and multiple piercings, her face was pale and regal. She wore a torn, camouflage miniskirt; a tight white tank revealed tattoos all over her peaches-and-cream arms. She was holding a snarling black poodle on a long leash, and I remembered that she'd thanked her dog, Kafka, on the acknowledgments page of *Bitter Ironies*.

James and I glanced at each other, open-mouthed. Without even really trying, we'd found our mystery writer.

"Uh, Philippa—are you Philippa Askance?" James blurted, jumping to his feet. I stood too, but my knees were shaking, so I almost slipped off the stoop.

"It's—it's really you," I stammered, gazing at the author, half awestruck, half distracted by James. "We were actually wondering if . . . you . . . might . . ." I trailed off, totally intimidated.

Philippa glanced from me to James, and the trace of a smile made her mouth twitch. Then, without a word, she sped down the steps past us, Kafka yapping. I watched in shock as writer and dog sprinted down the block, toward Prospect Park, and disappeared around the corner.

James and I stood alone on her stoop, probably looking like the biggest idiots alive.

Slowly, James turned to me. His face was as flushed as mine felt. "Did we, um, just imagine that?" he whispered.

I stared back at him. *Did I just imagine our almost-kiss?* I wanted to cry. I couldn't tell which event was more surreal.

"I don't think so," I managed to reply, hanging on to the banister for support. "It was definitely her."

"Well, uh, at least we know where she lives now." James shrugged, still looking flustered.

"If worse comes to worst we can always camp out on her stoop," I suggested, only semi-joking. "But she didn't seem all that friendly."

"Still, we should tell the group," James pointed out. "I'll e-mail everyone."

What were we doing? I wondered, my stomach clenching. Here we were, calmly discussing Philippa Askance, and completely ignoring the fact that *we'd been about to kiss!*

But what if James *hadn't* planned on kissing me? What if he was just leaning over to brush a leaf out of my hair, just like when Griffin wiped the coffee foam off my lip on Valentine's Day?

Suddenly, the sun went behind a cloud, and the temperature seemed to drop about twenty degrees. The wind blew and shook leaves down onto us. It felt almost like winter again. I shivered and reached down to pick up my jacket, slipping it over my shoulders as an unexpected lump formed in my throat. Our afternoon was over.

"Well, um, I should probably, you know, head home . . . ," James was saying, slowly backing away.

I started backing up too, in the opposite direction. "Right. Home."

Once I was safely around the corner, I broke into a run. My head was spinning from everything: Mrs. Ferber, our nonkiss, Philippa's mysterious smile, and James, James, James. Nothing made *any* sense, but I guess that was normal. I was falling in love, and there's no room for reason or logic in love's twisty tangles. I know that for a fact.

Or maybe that's a line from one of my romance novels.

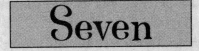 Seven

"You know, Norah," my mom said when we were clearing the dinner table on Thursday night. "I ran into Mrs. Ferber today, and she told me the funniest thing."

I'd been stuffing all the plates into the dishwasher at warp speed; I was eager to get upstairs and delve into my new Irene O'Dell paperback, *To Catch a Duke*, which I'd bought that afternoon at Barnes & Noble. However, at my mom's words, I dropped a handful of forks and straightened up.

"What did she say?" I asked, holding my breath as I recalled the awkward moment on the street.

"That she saw you with a cute boy," my

mom replied, putting an empty wineglass into the refrigerator as if it belonged there.

"Me?" I asked. "Not Stacey?"

"She seemed to think it was you," Mom replied, raising her eyebrows at me. "I mean, I *know* Stacey is usually the one with all the boyfriends . . ."

Thankfully, Stacey herself wasn't in the kitchen to hear this; she was at the movies with Dylan, again. My dad was in the living room, but he wouldn't have paid attention anyway.

I rolled my eyes and banged the salt cellar down on the counter. "Thanks, Mom. Why don't you rub some of this salt into my gaping wound?"

Ever since my dreamlike (or nightmarish; take your pick) encounter with James, I'd been moody and rude; Audre had started calling me "Ms. PMS." Even though I thought about James constantly—lying awake at night and reading love poetry during the day—we hadn't had any direct contact since that afternoon. He *had* sent a mass e-mail to the group—annoyingly titled "The Curious Incident of the Dog in the Day-Time"—which told the whole Philippa story, but naturally left off any mention of our almost-kiss. In other e-mails, Francesca, Neil, Scott, and Audre explained that they'd been in touch with Philippa's agent and editor, who were more helpful than the actual Philippa had been. In fact, the agent promised she'd get Philippa to commit to a date in May, about a month from now.

Standing in the kitchen, Mom looked at me over her glasses and sighed. "What wound? Norah, I don't understand you at all."

"Tell me about it," I replied, turning on my heel and storming out of the kitchen. Big surprise that my Mom didn't get my metaphor; scientists are the most literal people on the planet, and it sucks when your parent happens to be one.

Make that parents.

My dad was in his recliner, grading papers, so of course his hair was standing straight up and he had pencil marks on his face. All I had to do was make my way past him without tripping over his ten-thousand-pound textbook on thermonuclear neurodynamic physics (or something) and I'd be safely upstairs, curling up with *To Catch a Duke*.

Not in the cards.

"My dear, would you do me a favor?" Dad asked as I was sneaking by.

When my dad asks for a "favor," it usually involves agreeing to some scary experiment where he attaches plugs to your head. "I have a lot of homework," I replied, looking longingly up the stairs. That was true, but I wasn't planning to spend much time on it.

"I just need you to sprint up to the attic and pull my article on momentum out of last year's file," Dad said. "I'd do it myself, but the doctor told me to avoid the stairs as much as possible while I'm healing."

Okay, *now* I felt guilty. Last week in his seminar, Dad had thrown his back out after performing a headstand as a way of explaining the force of gravity. I supposed *To Catch a Duke* could wait a little longer.

Practically everything in the attic was buried under piles of dust. Between sneezes, I opened Dad's file cabinet and found a bulging folder labeled "Momentum"—which made me think of that great Aimee Mann song. I flipped through student exams but I stopped when I came to a glossy color photograph. A bunch of kids were standing in neat rows under a banner that read WINNERS OF THE COLUMBIA UNIVERSITY CITY-WIDE HIGH SCHOOL PHYSICS CONTEST. The winners' names were listed on the bottom of the photo. I remembered my dad attending the awards ceremony last spring, and I grinned at the sight of him; he and his hair were in the back row with the other judges.

Then, I spotted a face in the front row that made me gasp out loud.

"Neil!" I exclaimed, leaning closer to make sure. The glasses-wearing boy in the cableknit pullover was definitely the same sci-fi-reading Neil I'd come to know and not love. He wasn't bad-looking, I thought as I studied his face. All he needed were cooler frames and better social skills, and he might even qualify as a decent catch. Plus, he must have been a good student. My mom and dad *dreamed* that Stacey or I would win a physics contest, but that was about as likely as either one of us winning the pole vault in the summer Olympics.

My heartbeat sped up as I began to wonder if James might have won the contest too. He didn't strike me as the physics type, but since he and Neil seemed surgically attached . . . breathless, I scanned the captioned names on the bottom of the photo, looking for James's. There was Neil Singh, Hart Crane High School . . . George Woo, Bronx High School of Science . . . Francesca Cantone, Hamilton Preparatory School . . . Sigrid Salinger, Stuyvesant High School. No James Roth.

Wait. I did a double take on one name. Had I read that right? Francesca Cantone? *The* Francesca Cantone?

Insanely curious, I started searching the photo for Francesca's glossy hair and made-up face. When I spotted a tall, gawky girl in the next-to-last row, I squinted in disbelief. She had frizzy black hair pulled back in two barrettes, bushy eyebrows, and a slouchy posture. Round, chunky glasses perched on her nose, and she wore a white turtleneck under a frumpy navy blue cardigan. I mentally subtracted the clothes and the glasses, straightened and shortened the hair, plucked the brows . . .

"What the hell?" I whispered.

Clutching the photo in one hand, I found Dad's momentum article in a flash, dashed it downstairs to him, and then locked myself in my room, already dialing Audre's cell.

"Get over here right now," I said as soon as she answered.

"I'm baking for my party!" Audre cried over the strains of her Alicia Keys CD and the roar of her electric mixer.

Right. Audre was throwing her annual deluxe dessert party tomorrow. She always held her bash on the same night as Millay's Spring Formal, as an alternative for people (like me and her) who couldn't stand school dances. This was a touchy subject with Scott, who was actually *organizing* the dance this year. (The two of them had been competing over their respective events all week.) But Audre's parties are always best at the dances, and, even better, her parents leave her the brownstone for the night, so some crazy stuff usually goes down. Last year, Audre found a drunken couple she didn't even recognize making out in Langston's bedroom at six in the morning—the sign of a truly spectacular social event.

"Trust me, Aud," I assured her. "This is worth taking a break for." After all, I was putting off *To Catch a Duke*; Audre could part with her whipped cream.

Fifteen minutes later, Audre and I were hunkered down on my bed with the photo, a magnifying lens, and some freshly made cupcakes Audre had brought for me to taste-test for the party.

"Un-freaking-believable," Audre murmured, holding the magnifying lens over the photo for the eleventh time. "It *is* her. The real Francesca." My best friend was glowing.

"The weirdest thing," I said, pointing to Neil in the photo, "is that Mister Lord of the Rings won the same contest."

"Which explains why he asked if he knew her on the first day." Audre nodded. "But why did she ignore him?"

"*Obviously* she's *ashamed* of her geeky past. Wouldn't you be?" I reached for another cupcake. "Anyway, this explains so much: her going to Dartmouth, how she slipped up about that sci-fi book, why she's always so defensive. . . ."

Plus, I realized, Hamilton Prep is this snooty private school on the Upper West Side. Suddenly I remembered Francesca telling Scott that she went to school "uptown," but not offering more info. That, too, added up.

Audre was flashing her dimples uncontrollably. "I *almost* feel bad for how I've treated her. Imagine the stress of hiding a secret like that . . . not to mention all the painful eyebrow tweezing." She giggled, then glanced at me. "Oh my God! Do you think Griffin knows?"

"Probably not. Didn't she say they met this past fall? By then she must have fabuloused herself up. I mean, he *did* say she was smart, but come on—Griffin wouldn't go for her in that turtleneck, would he?"

Audre flapped the photo in the air. "I'm not one for blackmail, but—"

"Audre Antonia Legrand!" I threw a pillow at her.

"Joking," she said, tossing the photo down. "The mere *knowledge* of this puppy will make me *so* happy when I see her at the party tomorrow night."

"I can't believe you invited the whole group," I groaned. "I'm not emotionally prepared to see . . . well, you know."

Audre rolled her eyes. "Nors, you're

being silly. Just call James up and ask him out. Say 'I'd really like to get to know you better.' Or tell him you like him! Anything! Be proactive, baby." She leaned back against my pillows, still casting smiles down at the Francesca photo.

I let Audre's advice sink in. This was a novel idea for me. *Telling* the boy I liked that I . . . liked him? Madness! I'd never in a million years do it. Audre, on the other hand, is all about seizing the day. Except she doesn't always take her own advice. "Well, why don't *you* do something about Griffin?" I shot back.

Audre's cheeks reddened. "It's different. He's in college and all. And there's the whole *is-he-or-isn't-he?* with Francesca. But James is this, like, *reality*, Nors. He's kind of sexy—in a dorky way—he's practically your soul mate, and he clearly has some feelings for you—"

"Wrong on two counts," I cut in. "Maybe we connected over books, but that does *not* make him my soul mate." I knew I was lying even as I spoke. "Besides, I don't believe in that gushy stuff."

"Blah, blah, blah," Audre said.

"And he doesn't like me, Audre. I mean, he could've kissed me after Philippa left, right? Or e-mailed me. He had his chances." I sighed, my previous excitement about Francesca morphing into misery. "It's hopeless."

Audre snatched an uneaten cupcake from my hand. "I need that for tomorrow," she chided, then slung an arm around me. "Nors, believe me," she insisted. "You're making a mistake if you don't at least *try* to pursue James."

I knew she had a point; I wasn't going to get over James any time soon, and I was fed up with always pining after boys—with zero results.

"But I'm a total coward," I admitted with a shrug. "I won't make the first move. And I'm *awful* at flirting. So what am I supposed to do if I want to get him?"

After Audre left and I'd slogged through my homework, I washed up, changed into my pj's, and, at long last, climbed into bed with *To Catch a Duke*.

I lay back against my pillows and admired the cover: In a fancy ballroom, a dark-eyed girl with flowing brown hair, wearing a cream-colored gown, gazes into the intense blue eyes of a gentleman in riding breeches and a vest. I'm such a sucker for this stuff it worries me. Still, I'll take these books over *The Devil Wears Prada* any day. I'd read that earlier in the week, and had found it pretty vapid and shallow—the perfect choice for (the "new") Francesca.

Without wasting another second, I took a breath, opened *To Catch a Duke*, and dug in.

Dark-haired, slender Rosamund Billingsworth whirled about, tears pricking her amber-brown eyes. "It's not fair, Mother!" she cried in anguish. "Why should I suffer at the hands of love only because we are poor?"

"Yes, why?" I whispered, snuggling deeper under the covers, reading away.

The story went like this: Rosamund met Lorenzo, a hot blue-eyed Italian duke, at a neighbor's winter ball. They danced, flirted, and almost made out—but then Lorenzo blew her off big-time. A heart-broken Rosamund knew it was because of her pathetic social standing. So she decided to make Lorenzo fall hopelessly in love with her . . . by pretending to be the most desirable woman in all of England. Gripped by suspense, I read on as Rosamund concocted a range of ingenious man-getting schemes. But even as I was getting close to the end (and the clock was getting close to 4 a.m.), *nothing* seemed to be working—until Lorenzo discovered that Rosamund was pursuing his friend, Count Alberto:

"Oh, Rosamund," Lorenzo murmured, striding toward her with the same bold, manly confidence that had first caught her eye. His black hair glimmered in the sunlight and his piercing azure eyes burned. "If you love Alberto, I shall surely perish, for then there will be no hope in my universe."

"I do not love Alberto," Rosamund whispered, trembling at Lorenzo's impassioned words. "Nor any of the other men you have seen me with in town. It was all pretense."

Lorenzo stopped before her, and lightly brushed a finger across her ruby-red lips. "For whose benefit?" he asked, his voice smooth as satin.

"Yours," Rosamund confessed, her bosom heaving.

"And this," Lorenzo replied, sliding a strong arm about Rosamund's slim waist, "is for your benefit."

He lowered his head and ravaged her mouth

with a kiss so fiery Rosamund was certain she would melt. She returned his kiss, relishing the feel of his lips and his tongue, and the firm touch of his hands as they slid up and down her supple body. She wrapped herself around him as their kisses grew wilder, their hands more wanton.

Lorenzo reluctantly drew back, his breathing ragged. He caressed Rosamund's face, his eyes aflame with tenderness.

"Dear Rosamund," he whispered. "I cannot bear to see you with another man."

"There is no other man I want," Rosamund cried, "if you will have me—poor as I am."

"I care not a whit about your poverty or your name," Lorenzo declared, drawing her close. "Your beauty, your fierce spirit is worth all the wealth in the world. I love you, Rosamund. I will love you for all eternity."

"And I love you, Lorenzo," Rosamund sighed, collapsing in his arms once more.

"Marry me?" Lorenzo asked, holding her tightly.

"Today, if you wish," Rosamund murmured against his lips.

"Well," Lorenzo chuckled. "If that can't be arranged, perhaps you'll settle for an early honeymoon?"

And, under the sheltering branches of the leafy green trees, Lorenzo laid Rosamund against a soft blanket of grass. The lovers kissed and caressed as if they were ravenous, and finally consummated the pulsing desire that had simmered between them for so long.

I shut the book and fell back against my pillow, letting out a satisfied sigh. What an ending! Sure, the writing was a little flowery, but who cared? Rosamund was an awesome character—I totally admired her persistence when it came to going after the guy she wanted.

I sat up in bed, my heart thudding. *The guy she wanted. James.* Audre's words came back to me: *Be proactive, baby.* She was right. It was time to act. I'd been looking for the best way to pursue James, right? Now I had it, spelled out for me step-by-step by Irene O'Dell! Jealousy *is* powerful. All I had to do was convince James that I was the most wanted girl in New York City—and next time, he'd be sure to follow through on that kiss.

In a way, I realized, my skin flushing with inspiration, Mrs. Ferber may have helped me out by mentioning other boyfriends. James hadn't known she was talking about Stacey, so maybe he *already* suspected that I juggled twenty different boys.

Now I just had to confirm that suspicion.

Grabbing my journal, I stretched across my bed and took careful notes on each of Rosamund's stunts. They were as follows:

1) Before a lavish tea party, she wrote herself a love letter, disguising her handwriting (*Darling Rosamund, I must possess you*). At the party, Rosamund "accidentally" let the note fall out of her book of Shakespeare sonnets and onto Lorenzo's expensive shoe.

2) When her pushy parents invited Lorenzo to dine at their manor (I love how in these books, even the poor people live in mansions), Rosamund secretly arranged to have a lavish bouquet from an "admirer" delivered to her door.

3) While strolling in town with her brother-in-law, Rosamund ran into Lorenzo —and pretended said brother-in-law was really a suitor.

4) And finally, the icing on the cake: pretending to love Alberto.

Lying on my stomach, I chewed my pen cap, thinking hard. Weirdly enough, Rosamund's first step was practically already in place for me. Audre's dessert party tomorrow (well, today) was *almost* like a tea party. James would be there. I would be there. What better opportunity to let a love letter carelessly flutter to the ground?

And, best of all, since I didn't live in 1812, I wouldn't even have to disguise my sloppy handwriting. All I had to do was type!

My skin tingly, I slipped out of bed, bound my hair up in a messy bun, opened my iBook, and started writing.

Dearest, darling Norah—

Suddenly, I heard heavy footsteps thumping toward the bathroom in the hall and froze. It was Stacey; for someone so dainty, my sister walks like a baby elephant. I wondered if she'd seen the light on in my room, and for a second I felt like a criminal. An *insane* criminal. Who in their right mind wrote themselves a love letter?

Well, whatever. It worked for Rosamund.

When I heard Stacey return to her room, I let out a breath and went back to work.

Dearest, darling Norah,

How often have I admired your elegance and grace. I long for you deeply—

No. Horrible. I needed to stop channeling Irene O'Dell and make the letter sound like it came from a normal boy.

Hey N,

You might not know me, but I think you're smoking. Your ass looked so hot in those jeans today I almost—

Okay, but not a gross boy. Someone who'd actually go for me.

Norah,

This is kind of embarrassing, but I think you're one of the coolest girls I've ever known. And you're really cute, too.

I smiled, blushing. This was a nice self-esteem boost.

Figuring my made-up admirer should go to Millay, I added: *I'm in history class with you.* That sounded good; English would be too obvious. I kept going, feeling inspired.

You don't speak too often, but when you do, it's really smart. And when you take your dark hair out of its bun and let it swing down your back, I think it's, well, beautiful. Anyway, you probably have a boyfriend—girls like you are never single. If you think you know who this is, write me back, and tell me if I have a chance with you. I really, really hope so.

Faithfully yours,

An admirer

I reread the note on my screen, biting my nails and reviewing the works. The letter seemed to work. It was the right mix of shy-boy awkward and smart-boy poetic. Exactly the kind of love letter I would want to receive. And, hopefully, the kind that would completely fool James.

The early sunlight was painting my walls gold as I printed the letter, folded it, and carefully tucked it into *my* copy of Shakespeare sonnets, which I'd take to Audre's house that night. Giving up on sleep, I headed out the door for the shower, mentally preparing myself for what lay ahead. Depending on how things went, this could very well be the best night of my life. Or the worst.

Eight

Trying to stay awake, I slipped a Modest Mouse CD into Audre's player and turned the volume way up just as Audre bumped into me from behind, almost dropping her tray of mini éclairs.

"Watch it!" she cried over the opening chords of the first track. "You're supposed to be helping, *not* ruining everything."

"Sorry," I replied, but it came out as a yawn. Then I stepped out of her warpath. Audre turns into a bit of a lunatic when she's setting up for a party. I watched as she stomped toward the table in her purple satin pumps and added the éclairs to the mouth-watering spread of goodies and drinks. The bottles of wine on the table were courtesy of Langston, who'd bought them for Audre the last time he was home. He's the best.

"Isn't Langston just the best?" I heard Audre's mom, Mrs. Legrand, say. "He reserved us a room at the hotel in New Haven." She was floating regally down the stairs, and Mr. Legrand was behind her, carrying their bags. They were going to visit Langston at Yale that weekend, conveniently leaving the brownstone to Audre for the party. Needless to say, the Legrands are very cool in this way; my parents would barely understand what a "party" was, let alone let me throw one alone in the house.

The Legrands are only *not* cool when they're shooting down Audre's dreams of her own pastry empire. Which was happening that very moment.

"Honey, this looks lovely, but perhaps you've gone overboard," Mrs. Legrand was saying, hands on her impressive hips as she met Audre at the table. Audre is curvy in a cute/sexy way, but Mrs. Legrand looks as if she may have enjoyed one too many mini éclairs. She swept her chubby, chocolate-colored hand across the living room and sighed dramatically. After school that day, Audre and I had strung white and silver streamers and lit cinnamon-scented candles; the place was absolutely party-ready. "I hope you took some time to finish your homework," Mrs. Legrand added worriedly.

"Mom, it's Friday," Audre grumbled, smoothing out the glittery white tablecloth she'd sewn herself. "I'll do it on Sunday at midnight, like always."

Mr. Legrand, who is as short and thin as Mrs. Legrand is, well, grand and imposing, cleared his throat as he walked by Audre with the bags. "That's not a wise idea, Audre. You know what an important time of year this is. I'm sure Norah is doing all she can to prepare for college." He turned to beam at me and I blushed. It's a rule: Parents pretty much always seem to prefer your best friend to you.

I shrugged. "Well, not really," I mumbled, feeling guilty. It was true that, since starting the book group, I'd felt more inspired to get all my homework done and even—*shudder*—study a little more. But I still wasn't exactly a role model for college prep.

After Audre's parents left, calling over their shoulders that we shouldn't break anything, Audre stormed back toward the kitchen, fuming.

"Homework," she muttered to herself. "That's the *last* thing on my mind! I have to make sure my pies haven't burned before the guests arrive."

I also had other—but different—things on my mind. My book of Shakespeare sonnets—fake love letter included—was sitting on the coffee table, worrying me. While Audrea and I had been decorating that afternoon, I'd spilled the whole Rosamund scheme to my best friend. When I was finished, Audre had put down her streamer, raised one eyebrow, and asked, "You *do* realize how much can go wrong?"

So now I was worried *and* dead tired. A tip: When you're about to go after the boy of your dreams, do not—I repeat, do not—stay up all night. I felt like a zombie and didn't think I looked much better, even in my favorite green belted dress and cowboy boots.

I was reaching down to pick up the

book of sonnets—just to make sure my note was doing okay—when the doorbell rang. "Nors, can you get it?" Audre hollered from the kitchen. Assuming it was Tuesday or Olivia—or maybe even Scott, sneaking away from the Spring Formal—I tucked the book under my arm and hurried across the living room.

"Who's up for a party?" I asked, flinging the door open.

My entire book group was standing on Audre's doorstep.

"Uh, I am?" Neil offered, grinning. He seemed more relaxed than usual, and didn't look half bad, in a yellow Polo shirt and jeans. He gestured to Francesca, Griffin, and (gulp) James beside him. "Hope it's cool we all came together." Neil added. "I figured you, Audre, and Scott would do your own thing, so I e-mailed everyone else."

"That's fine," I said, my cheeks already hot. *No! Not fine!* James wasn't supposed to show up *now*. I needed more time to rehearse and get tipsy on white wine before I whipped out some love letter action.

Then I noticed that there were a few new faces among the four I already knew.

Standing next to Griffin was a petite girl with a shiny black bob, short bangs, and pearl-framed vintage-y glasses. She had the hipster look of most NYU students, so I figured she was a college friend—or more, perhaps? Standing behind James was a chubby, teddy bear-ish boy who I recognized from the pool game James had pointed out at Art House.

"This is our friend Theo," Neil said, pointing to the new guy as everyone came inside.

I nodded, smiling, but Theo was too busy staring at Francesca, his tongue practically hanging out of his mouth.

Francesca had also brought a friend along; she was linking arms with a girl who had a mass of curly dark blond hair and wore a metallic silver strapless dress under a furry black shrug—a Plum all the way.

"And this is *my* friend," Francesca said smugly, stepping past me into the foyer. "Mimi."

Mimi rolled her eyes as a way of saying hello. "Why did you drag me out to Brooklyn?" I heard her whine to Francesca, who immediately starting apologizing.

I can't even tell you how freaky it was to see Francesca at her most glam—silky, spaghetti-strap tank, sleek cropped black pants, long silver earrings—and remember the awkward girl in the photo. Were they really the same person? How had she changed so much? And why? I observed Francesca carefully as she followed Mimi to the food table, asking, "What can I get you?" in a breathless voice. It was obvious Mimi was the queen bee, and Francesca her little lapdog. Audre was going to *love* seeing Francesca act so wussy.

And then I got it—or at least some of it: Mimi must have been a brand-new friend, part of the trendy crowd Francesca had fought to join after she'd shed her turtlenecks and glasses—and, most likely, her old friends. I suddenly recognized Francesca's type—we had them at Millay, too: Wannabe Plums, girls who'd managed to pull themselves out of the unpopular pit but still remained on the outskirts of the cool clique. It made me feel almost sorry for Francesca; there had to be heaps of insecurity beneath her bitchy attitude.

"Here ya go, Norah," Griffin said,

breaking into my thoughts and handing me a six-pack of Stella Artois. "This is Eva, a friend of mine from school," he added, lightly touching the petite, dark-haired girl on the small of her back. She nodded at me. *So she is an NYU student,* I thought. But was she really just a "friend"? Hmm. With Griffin, one never knew. I'd have to alert Audre about this latest development.

"I'm glad you could make it," I told Griffin truthfully, accepting the beer. Audre had been crushed when her crush had replied to her Evite with a "maybe," claiming he had to cram for an art history exam. His being here would make her night, *even* if this Eva chick *was* in the picture.

He shrugged. "Hey, dude. Naturally. I couldn't pass up this chance to see—" He suddenly stopped, like he didn't want to say anything else. His sun-kissed face flushed a little and he glanced down. Was ever-cool Griffin . . . *blushing?*

To see who? I wondered. It had to be Audre. Maybe he *did* like her! I felt a spark of excitement. But if that was the case, why would he bring another girl to her party?

"So where are your other thirds?"

Griffin asked as Eva—who hadn't said a word—wandered off toward the food table.

"You mean Audre and Scott?" I asked, laughing. "Aud is off being the perfect hostess. And Scott's at our rival event—Millay's Spring Formal." I made a face and Griffin chuckled.

"Listen, I should go find Eva," he said, squeezing my arm in his patented *I'm-not-really-flirting-with-you-am-I?* Griffin way. "You'll have to excuse her. She's—get this—not supposed to talk for a full weekend as part of this performance art class she's taking. When I told a bunch of my friends about this party, Eva said she wanted to come along to 'challenge' herself." Griffin made air quotes with his fingers and crinkled up his perfect, freckly nose.

I nodded, curious. I agreed with Griffin's cynical take on Eva's whole vow-of-silence act, but I wondered: If he *was* dating Eva, would he poke fun at her like that? It didn't seem to be Griffin's style. But before I could find out the truth, the doorbell rang again. And again. Kids started pouring in and soon the party was in full swing, everyone sampling Audre's treats, gossiping in big circles, and dancing in small groups throughout the living room.

For the first hour, I was busy catching up with the friends I'd had less time for since the book group began. Sipping sparkling white wine, I listened as Ha-Jin and Stephanie—assistant editors on the yearbook—complained about layouts and pesky photographers, and a newly recovered Olivia described the hellishness of mono. Tuesday, it turned out, was back on the outs with her boy toy—at least until he flew her to Cabo again. As we were wrapping up our chat, my eyes roamed across the room until I saw James. He was sitting on the Legrands' sofa, eating a mini éclair alongside Francesca, Neil, and Theo. He didn't see me.

Now or never. My pulse racing, I told Tuesday and the other girls that I had "something important" to do. Then I finished my glass of wine in a gulp. I'm not a big drinker, and that combined with zero sleep made my head feel very fuzzy—which maybe wasn't a bad thing. Praying to Rosamund for strength, I walked across the living room with the book still under my arm and sat in an armchair facing the sofa.

James lifted his chin toward me in, yes, another one of those frustrating boy nods. I nodded back, noticing how his blue shirt matched his eyes. "Hey, Norah, we were just talking about Philippa Askance," he said shortly. He didn't smile or in any way show that he remembered our moment in front of her house. I was much too antsy to respond.

"Her agent says she's crazy," Neil chimed in, balancing an empty plate on his lap. "Like, she promises to do lots of readings but always bails at the last minute."

"I heard that too," Theo added as he not-too-subtly tried to peek down Francesca's silky top.

"Let's hope that doesn't happen to us," I finally managed to say, thinking that, at this point, the Philippa reading was the only thing holding our group together.

Meanwhile, Francesca was giving me a slow, snotty once-over, definitely scrutinizing my outfit.

"Where's Mimi?" I asked her, putting my Shakespeare book in my lap. *Aren't you lost without your leader?* I wanted to add.

Francesca pointed to the far corner. "There," she said curtly.

I turned to see Mimi on a love seat, seriously fooling around with Jorge Marquez, one of Derek Dawson's hot soccer friends. Derek himself was standing next to the love seat, looking depressed as he gazed around the living room; he was probably searching for Audre.

"Oh," I said, facing Francesca again. So *that* was why she was stuck over on the couch with the dynamic trio of Neil, James, and Theo. But why wasn't she with Griffin? Unless he was off making out with Eva (she wouldn't have to break her vow of silence for *that*). Oh, God. I could just imagine Audre finding the two of them in Langston's bedroom. That would be, well, not fun.

Francesca narrowed her eyes at the Shakespeare in my lap. "Norah, Norah, Norah," she said, and then giggled. "You accessorized with a book! You know, you strike me as just the kind of girl who would do that."

Really? And you strike me as just the kind

of girl who would win the Columbia University City-Wide High School Physics Contest but then pretend you're a ditz.

Audre would have said that, but I held back.

And realized that Francesca had just given me my opening.

I held up the book, hoping to seem casual even though my knees were semi-knocking together. "My Shakespeare sonnets? Yeah, I carry this around with me sometimes just, you know—for inspiration." This was a lie; I'd had to read some sonnets for English class last year, but hadn't spend much time with Shakespeare since. As I spoke, I gave the book a little shake. My letter didn't budge.

"Shakespeare sonnets?" James echoed, giving me a funny look.

"Ooh, read one out loud!" Francesca gushed. "It'll be *sooo* romantic." Was it my imagination or was she making googly eyes at . . . Neil? Or maybe Theo—I couldn't tell. She must have been drunk, I figured, or trying to make Griffin jealous—wherever he was.

Did I have a choice? My fingers trembling, I flipped through the pages until I came to a random sonnet.

I read: "'Let me not to the marriage of true minds—'" Theo snickered, but I kept going: "'Admit impediments. Love is not love which alters—'"

I stopped, blushing. "Forget it," I muttered, hurriedly turning the page. Bad choice. Saying the word "love" in front of, well, the boy you love is a tad embarrassing. But as I hurriedly turned the page in search of another sonnet, my stubborn letter *finally* slipped out and tumbled to the floor.

It landed on the toe of my cowboy boot, so I gave it a discreet kick and it shot across the rug, stopping at the heels of James's Skechers. Goal!

Too bad you can't play soccer with love letters; I might actually be a good athlete, then.

James didn't notice the letter. Nobody did. It sat there, a little white square of paper, waiting for its big moment. *Look down!* I silently urged James, but he was busy with his mini éclair. I barely listened as Francesca babbled on about her recent trip to Bloomingdale's. Then I heard her say, "Do you think another cupcake will make me *fat*?" She pinched her nonexistent hips and pouted at Neil and Theo, who were both about to drool. She must have adored tormenting boys like them.

"Nope," Theo said, jumping to his feet.

"Not at all," Neil added, leaping up too. This was obviously going to be a race to the food table. But Neil had shot up so fast that he dropped his plate with a clatter. When he knelt down to pick it up, he glanced at the paper next to James's shoe. "Did someone lose a napkin?" he asked, his brow furrowing.

And then reached for letter.

Yes, I should have said. *That's* my *napkin.* I should have jumped up and snatched the letter from Neil's grasp.

But instead I sat there, girl-in-the-headlights, wondering in terror where this was going to lead. I hadn't once stopped to consider that someone *other* than James might pick up the love letter.

But maybe it didn't matter. Maybe Neil would only glance at the note and hand it over to James and everything would happen just as Irene O'Dell had intended.

It didn't work out that way.

Neil stood up slowly, unfolding the note, and his dark eyes skimmed down the letter. He glanced up at me and his face broke into a wicked smile. I felt fear climbing up my chest, into my throat, silencing me.

"No . . . *way*," Neil whispered. "This is for *you*, Norah!"

Finally, I kicked myself into action. "That fell out of my book, Neil," I stammered, stumbling to my feet and reaching for the note. "Give it back."

In classic elementary school style, Neil held the letter over his head. "Nuh-uh. Come and get it!"

Theo laughed. A few kids sitting on a nearby couch glanced over curiously, and I heard a girl giggle. My stomach twisted; this wasn't looking promising.

"Ooh, read it out loud!" Francesca cried, for the second time that night. I wondered if her extreme makeover had seriously limited her vocabulary.

More people, sniffing out potential gossip, started drifting over. Even Mimi and Jorge stopped groping each other to watch the action. I heard murmurs of "What's going on?" and "Something with Norah." I remained paralyzed, watching Neil, not letting myself breathe. Turning around to look at James—or anyone else—was out of the question.

Neil cleared this throat, held the note to his face, and began: "'Norah, this is kind of embarrassing, but I think you're one of the coolest girls I've ever known. And you're pretty cute, too.'" He paused to chuckle. I cringed at the words I'd written in the privacy of my room—words meant for James's eyes only. Audre had been right. This was all going so, so wrong. Laughter and whispers buzzed around me. "It's a secret admirer!" someone said, and somebody else turned off the music, the better for Neil to perform. And Neil kept performing, reading in a loud, clear voice, adding gestures for emphasis, obviously loving the spotlight. I'd always thought Neil was shy, but now that he had this chance to mortify me, he seemed to be blossoming right before my eyes.

The bastard.

By the time he got to the classic "girls

like you are never single" line, most of the party was squished into the living room and I was enjoying a very pleasant out-of-body experience. I floated somewhere above the crowd, feeling very, very sorry for the dumb girl in the green dress and cowboy boots.

"Excuse me—let me through—what's going on here?—this is *my* party!"

I turned around, practically fainting with relief at the sound of Audre's voice.

My peeved-looking best friend was elbowing her way through the crush of people. When she saw me, and Neil holding the letter, and the crowd, her eyes widened and her mouth dropped open. She gave me a look that was half *I'm so sorry* and half *I told you so*.

"Norah, who do you think it's from?" Olivia was crying from the other side of the room. "Maybe he's here tonight!"

"Yeah!" Ha-Jin called out. "Hey, if you're Norah's secret lover, raise your beer!" There was more laughter.

"This is ludicrous," Audre sputtered, storming up to Neil and yanking the letter from his hand. "Neil, I think the bus to the local *kindergarten* is waiting outside for you," she snapped. Then, rolling her eyes, she turned to the rest of the crowd and made a *shoo!* motion with her floury hands. "Show's over, peeps. Would someone please turn the music back on so we can return to our regularly scheduled party?"

What would I do without this girl?

The crowd thinned out. Mimi and Jorge started kissing again. The Futureheads CD came back on. My love letter was forgotten— at least for the moment. I threw my arms gratefully around Audre. She hugged me back, hard, stuffing the doomed love letter into my hand.

"It's over," she said firmly, pulling away.

"Where *were* you?" I asked, still shaking.

Audre frowned. "Recovering from Griffin. He came up to me in the kitchen with this weird girl who refused to speak, and then he just *left*. He gave me a hug good-bye and told me he had to go study da Vinci."

Then Audre glanced over my shoulder and her face lit up. *Is Griffin back?* Still a little unsteady, I turned around and saw Scott walking through the door, looking sheepish in his confetti-sprinkled, wrinkled tux. Of course. I knew he'd choose Audre's bash over the Spring Formal eventually.

"So," Audre said, crossing her arms over her chest in triumph as Scott loped over. "Look who the cat dragged in."

Scott grinned and wrapped his arm around my waist. "All right, all right. You win. I couldn't bear to be apart from my girls for *too* long. Besides," he sighed. "Despite my endless hours of planning, the formal was a total letdown. Think, like, Usher slow jams, tasteless fruit punch, and Plum and her cronies in matching Trina Turk dresses." Then he paused, clearly noticing the traumatized expression on my face. "Oh, God. What did I miss *here*?"

By now, Scott was more than aware of my James crush, but didn't yet know the Rosamund details. I started to tell him—maybe he'd be able to give me a helpful boy perspective—when Audre suddenly glanced over my shoulder again and promptly grabbed Scott's arm. Yanking him away, she told me, "Norah, we have to go. See you later."

And then she and Scott darted off past me.

My heart sank. Why were my best friends

abandoning me in my time of need?

"You guys, come back!" I cried, spinning around.

And I found myself face-to-face with James.

Okay, *that* was why they'd left.

"Um, hi," James said, hands in his pockets, hair in his eyes, as always. My pulse spiked. "Listen, I'm sorry about what Neil just did. He can be——" James shrugged. "Immature." At James's words, I glanced around and saw Neil back at the food table, talking to Francesca and Theo. "He's not a bad guy, though," James added.

I nodded, loving James even more. So he *was* sweet, somewhere underneath that aloof attitude.

"Oh, whatever. It was funny," I lied, crumpling up the letter in my fist as if it were garbage.

James studied the carpet, his ears red. "So . . . who *do* you think gave it to you?" he asked. Then he looked up and flashed his crooked grin.

I almost gasped. After all that humiliation, had the stupid letter actually . . . done its job? I barely dared believe it, but James seemed intrigued—by *me*! Irene O'Dell was a goddess!

I tried to bat my lashes—I'd never done it before so I may have messed it up—and said, "Hmm. I'm not sure. I got it in school this morning, so really, it might be lots of guys . . ."

Rosamund herself couldn't have said it better.

James nodded, and it looked for a second like he wanted to laugh—but not in a mean way. Still, I decided to quit while I was ahead. I told James I needed to get a drink—which I did kind of need right then—and headed toward the kitchen. I also needed to find Audre and tell her that things hadn't gone so wrong after all.

And I needed to figure out what kind of bouquet to send myself for when I next saw James.

It was time for step two.

Nine

"Good morning, Park Slope Florist. How may I help you?"

"I'm just calling to—ouch—confirm a delivery," I said as an empty can of oatmeal landed on my foot. My hands were full, so I tossed *To Catch a Duke* down on the counter. "A bouquet of roses for Norah Bloom? Today at eleven thirty?"

"Got it," the woman chirped. "Bloom, Eighth Street. We'll be there."

"Thanks!" I said, clicking off and almost spilling a box of stale Cheerios all over myself. I was on a step stool, hunting through our kitchen cabinets for stuff to feed the book group.

A week ago Griffin had e-mailed us to say that there was a reading at the Book Nook on the same day as our *The Devil Wears Prada* meeting, so the café would be closed to the public, and Griffin had to work double shifts. Seeing an incredible opportunity for my second Rosamund plan, I invited the group to my house for a Saturday brunch. Plus, since I had that week off for spring break—which Audre and I, boringly, spent going shopping, renting cheesy romantic comedies, and studying for our SATs—I'd had time to review my Rosamund notes, order my secret-admirer flowers, *and* beg Stacey and my parents that they stay out of my hair while the group was here.

But I'd forgotten about the minor detail of *food*. I am so not like Audre.

I glanced at my watch: It was ten o'clock, and the meeting was supposed to start at eleven. There was plenty of time to run out to the corner deli and pick up a few things.

Twenty harried minutes later I was on line, waiting to pay for my bagels, cream cheese, and cherry tomatoes, when I noticed a familiar figure ahead of me. Spiky bleached hair, tattoos, torn overalls, combat boots. My breath caught.

"Philippa!" I whispered. Again! What were the chances? I looked around at the other customers; no one else in the store seemed to notice that a famous writer was standing about two feet away. I rose up on my tiptoes and tried to peek into her food basket; what did Philippa Askance *eat*? I wondered if she was a vegetarian like me, and I grinned at the thought.

But I couldn't make out her purchases, because by then she was paying. I felt a stab of panic; I didn't want her to leave yet! If I could get Philippa's attention now, this might be my big chance to redeem myself for that last embarrassing encounter in front of her house. And if I actually spoke to her, it would make a great story for James—and the others.

Clutching her bags, Philippa headed out the electronic doors. Without thinking too much about it, I dumped my basket on a crate—I could come back later—and tore out of the store. Feeling like a stalker, I trailed the punk poet down Seventh Avenue.

I could tell, from the fast, almost nervous way she walked, that Philippa Askance was insanely shy; I almost saw a bit of *myself* in her. Her shyness would explain why she was such a hermit, even if it didn't match the fearless and raw voice in *Bitter Ironies*. Maybe writers' personalities don't always fit with how you imagine them from their books.

That's it, I realized. *Bitter Ironies*—that was how I could get Philippa to talk to me! I'm always less timid when I can start off talking about books; somehow I sensed Philippa would be the same.

I walked faster until I was right behind her and forced myself to speak. "'Under the lemon moon / So bitter / I hide in the shadows / Haunted by memory,'" I quoted, remembering a few of my favorite lines from her book. This was maybe the bravest—and stupidest—thing I'd ever done. Not counting the fake love letter, of course.

Philippa stopped walking, turned around, and snapped off her shades. Her eyes were so dark blue they were almost purple, and she blinked them at me. I froze, wishing I'd thrown on something funkier than torn jeans and a Brooklyn Dodgers T-shirt. It was too bad Audre and I had chickened out when we went to get our noses pierced in the East Village last summer; maybe Philippa would think I was cooler if I had some face jewelry.

To my surprise, Philippa smiled at me. "Thanks," she whispered. "I like that part a lot."

"Me too. Well, I like the whole book." I laughed nervously. "I, um, can't wait for the next one." *I am talking to Philippa Askance!*

She studied me for a second. "I know you," she said quietly.

"You do?" I gulped.

Philippa nodded. "You and a boy were sitting outside my house about a month ago. You tried to talk to me?" She shook her head, biting her pierced bottom lip. "I'm sorry. I get weird about stuff like that. I'm more of a one-on-one person, you know?"

"I can relate," I said, then I shook *my* head. "I mean, I'm not famous or anything so I can't really. . . ." I blushed, telling myself to shut up.

Philippa smiled again, her dark blue eyes thoughtful. "I understand." She shifted her bags to her other arm. "So what did you guys want to say?" she asked, sounding curious. I was surprised at how much this felt like talking to a friend. Quickly, I explained about our book group's mission, and how we'd been in touch with her agent, and she nodded.

"I remember now," Philippa murmured. "My agent e-mailed me. The high school book group. The end of May, at the Book Nook. Just a reading, right?"

"Actually," I said, getting a crazy idea. (What can I say? I'm known for those.) "Maybe you could also, like, guest-star at our meeting! You know, we'd have the reading, and then the book group could meet afterward to discuss *Bitter Ironies*? And you'd be there to answer our questions!" I nodded, proud of my amazing initiative. Ms. Bliss would be so impressed.

But Philippa didn't seem too impressed. She seemed . . . scared. She cleared her throat, hesitating, and even took a few steps back from me.

Damn. I'd probably gone overboard. "Um," I covered. "I guess we can think about that part. But you *will* be able to come to the reading, right?" I held my breath, worried Philippa would change her mind.

She slipped her shades back on and tilted

her head to the side, back in mystery mode. "I'll be there in some form," she replied softly. "I promise."

Huh?

"I should go," Philippa said. She took a couple more steps back, and raised one hand. "I need to run home and write."

Of course—her writing! I imagined Philippa returning to her brownstone and walking upstairs with her groceries. Maybe she'd pet Kafka and then settle down at her gigantic desk, open her laptop with a flourish, and begin typing her new masterpiece. *That* was the last thing I wanted to keep Philippa Askance from. So, still feeling surreal after our talk, I nodded, waved back, and turned to go.

"Hey, wait," Philippa called after me. "Are you still with that boy?"

I looked over my shoulder, confused. "What bo—" I began, and then realized. *James.* Philippa Askance thought I was . . . *with* James. She'd seen us together and assumed we were a couple! That had to mean something, didn't it? (True, Mrs. Ferber had assumed the same thing, but whatever.)

"Oh, that boy? We're not together," I

replied truthfully, gazing sadly at the side-walk.

Philippa sighed. "Really? You guys were . . . adorable. You both gave off this vibe of—" She paused and I could tell she was trying to think up the perfect words like I did sometimes. "Innocent abandon."

Innocent abandon? I wasn't entirely sure what that meant, but it sounded very poetic. And it was about *me and James*!

Suddenly, I remembered James, my Rosamund flower delivery, and the book group. I glanced at my watch—it was almost eleven; I'd never have time to pick up the food from the grocery store now. I needed to bid Philippa adieu and race home as quickly as possible.

But when I looked up to tell the mysterious poetess good-bye, she was already gone.

I arrived at my brownstone, with a stitch in my side and my ponytail unraveling, to find the whole book group waiting on my stoop, looking impatient.

My parents were both working that day, and Stacey was upstairs, sleeping off the screaming match she'd had with her boyfriend the night before, so nobody had answered the doorbell. Apologizing—and trying not to think the words "innocent abandon" every time I looked at James—I unlocked the door and ushered the group inside.

Audre and Scott, who were as tight as ever now that the Spring Formal was over, walked in side by side, looking stressed. At school last week, I'd finally given Scott the whole Rosamund rundown, and he'd been super-supportive, not even remembering to mock me for my secret romance novel passion. Both he and Audre were well aware of today's planned flower fake-out. In fact, I'd asked that both my friends play a role in the scheme, and, last night, we'd even rehearsed our lines over three-way calling. This time, I'd decided, there was going to be *no* messing up.

Francesca sauntered into my house with barely a hello, sporting giant sunglasses, a silky draped top, slim Bermuda shorts and wedge-heeled espadrilles—clearly, she was getting into fashionable character for her big *The Devil Wears Prada* moment. I still couldn't help wanting to shout: *I know the truth!* at her, but, right then, I was too busy with my own dramas.

James and Neil were the last to enter, and they both observed my living room with interest, staring at the science textbooks on the shelves. "Whoa," Neil whispered, obviously impressed—it occurred to me that my parents would love him—while James ran a hand through his hair and murmured a more thoughtful, "Wow."

"What?" I asked James, feeling slightly defensive, while the rest of the group headed for the kitchen.

James turned toward me, half-shrugging as we cut across the living room together. "Well, it's just that—you're really different from your parents, right?"

You think?

I grinned, flattered that James had bothered to notice, and was about to agree wholeheartedly when I noticed him do a double take at something on the cluttered coffee table. Following his gaze, I felt my skin freeze.

No!

There, on top of a stack of old newspapers, sat *To Catch a Duke*.

That morning, before calling the florist, I'd thumbed through the book while standing in the kitchen—rereading Rosamund's bouquet scene for inspiration. Then, while dashing out the door to the grocery store, I'd absentmindedly tossed the book onto the coffee table, figuring I'd spirit it up to my room when I returned. Of course, that hadn't happened, so my gigantic secret was lying there, in plain view, for the whole world—and James—to see.

I was getting ready to snatch the book off the table—or explain myself somehow—but, to, my relief, James glanced away and continued toward the kitchen, unruffled.

I made myself breathe steadily. In. Out. In. Out. So James had seen a romance novel in my living room. Big deal. He didn't have to automatically assume it belonged to me. And, most importantly, he had no way of knowing that I was taking serious love advice from said book.

Still, I'd have to make sure to stash Rosamund and Co. back upstairs as soon as humanly possible.

In the kitchen, I laid out my humble food offerings—dry cereal, peanut butter, and toast—to the grumbles of "Oh, man, that's *it*?" and "I knew we should've gone to a diner" and "Norah, have I taught you nothing?" (that was Audre, of course). But I didn't feel too guilty—I had the mother of all excuses.

"Well, I *was* standing in line to get tastier stuff," I explained huffily as we all settled down around the butcher-block table. "But that mission kind of got put on hold when I saw, oh yeah, *Philippa freaking Askance*."

An excited hush fell over the table, so I eagerly told the whole story—from my minor stalking, to my obsessive-fan quoting, to the weird but wonderful conversation. I could feel James watching me, but though the others gave me enthusiastic props for my bravery, he remained silent. I wondered if he was envious that *he* hadn't had been the one to chat up his beloved Philippa.

"So it's set," über-organized Scott declared, checking the planner in his T-Mobile Sidekick. "The *Bitter Ironies* meeting is gonna be at the end of May, and then we're all on summer vacation, right? Does everyone already have summer plans?"

"Yeah," I sighed, forgetting Philippa for

a moment. "My glamorous shelving job at the local library starts in June."

Summers were always the same for me: weekdays spent at the library—reading the books when I was supposed to be shelving them—and weekends spent wandering around Prospect Park, getting a sunburn on my arms and neck and wishing that *this* would be the summer I'd fall in love. Or at least have a fling—that seemed to be a summer trend among a lot of my friends. It hadn't happened to me yet.

James smiled, almost to himself. "I'll be interning at an independent book publisher in the neighborhood." He said this modestly, but I realized how surprisingly together James was. *He* probably would have no trouble getting into college.

"I applied to work at Ozzy's," Audre offered anxiously between bites of toast. Ozzy's is this other mellow writers-and-lattes café in the Slope, and Audre had recently auditioned for an assistant baker position in their kitchen. She hadn't heard yet, but getting the job would score her big points with her skeptical parents.

"Art camp in July for me," Scott

chimed in, pretending to be annoyed—but I knew he secretly loved it.

"Science day camp for me." Neil grinned —he made no bones about loving *that*.

We all looked at Francesca, who was playing with the emerald ring on her finger. "Packing for Dartmouth," she replied shortly. I wondered if she had other plans— perhaps ones that involved her Physics Girl past—but I wasn't about to ask.

"Anyway," Scott said, anally going back to his planner, "does that mean the May meeting will be our last?"

Our *last*! My throat tightened.

The others nodded, looking as depressed as I felt. Which was bizarre.

Sure, the six of us had *sort of* bonded since February. After the Great Geek Discovery, Audre had been downright, well, *polite* to Francesca. And everyone else's tension also seemed to have lessened, making us feel almost like . . . friends. But I knew that wasn't why I was crushed to end the book group. Without our monthly meetings—and the Philippa hunt—I'd most likely never see James again. And Audre, similarly, was upset because she'd miss seeing so much of Griffin. But what was everyone else's problem?

Unless they *all* had a different hidden agenda keeping them loyal to the group.

But that would be way too freaky.

We'd just started discussing *The Devil Wears Prada* ("What was everyone's favorite outfit description?" Francesca asked, in all seriousness) when my doorbell rang. Audre and Scott immediately glanced at me, looking as wide-eyed and worried as I suddenly felt.

The flowers had arrived.

"I wonder who that could be!" I exclaimed, trying not to cringe at how fake I sounded. Have I mentioned what a heinous actress I am? Excusing myself from the table, I hurried out of the kitchen, racing to the front door in the living room.

"Bloom?" the delivery boy asked from behind a quivering mountain of red roses.

I took a deep breath. I hate roses; I'd wanted to get something more unusual, like a tiger-lily-and-lilac bouquet. But I couldn't afford be subtle here. Things had to be as clear as possible: *Lots of boys like me!*

I barely looked at the sheet the delivery

boy gave me—I just signed and then lugged the heavy vase into the kitchen.

"Wow," Francesca said. "*Somebody's spending the big bucks on you, Norah.*"

James sat up straighter, and Neil, probably feeling guilty about what he'd done at Audre's party, said nothing.

So far, so good.

"Hey, who are they from?" Audre asked, delivering her line perfectly as I set the vase on the counter.

"I have no clue!" I giggled, hoping to sound overwhelmed by my zillions of admirers.

When I'd placed my order with the florist I'd asked that the card come from a "Sebastian" (I'd picked the name randomly from one of Irene O'Dell's books). Now, I plucked the small white card out of the bouquet, expecting to see "Sebastian's" message (*Norah,* mon amour—*you fill me with passion. These flowers are as stunning as you are. Kisses, Sebastian*). Instead, this is what the card said:

Stacey, baby. I'm SO sorry about last night. Girl, will u ever forgive me? I luv u. Dylan.

Oh . . . God. This wasn't my bouquet at

all. I pictured my sister's boyfriend—gelled blond hair, clear braces, boy-band fashion sense. Of course Dylan would send Stacey roses—he had no imagination.

I chewed on the pad of my thumb, wondering what to do. I *could* just fess up the sad truth: My little sister had a better love life than I ever would. But I hadn't yet received *my* delivery, and I was worried the florist might have messed up and forgotten. At least I had *some* flowers now. And Stacey was sound asleep; she'd never know the difference.

I went for it.

"They're from Sebastian," I told the group, my face hot. I stuffed the card into my jeans pocket, hoping no one would ask to see it.

"Is this the same guy who sent you the other note?" Scott asked, right on cue, clearly not aware anything was wrong.

"Nope," I replied after a beat, channeling Rosamund. *You are the most wanted girl in New York City.* "I was already going out with Sebastian when I got that letter."

"You were?" Francesca piped up, looking suspicious. "Why didn't you bring him to the party?"

Oh, what a tangled web we weave. "Well—we're not that serious," I fudged, looking at Scott and Audre for help. But then, thankfully, I was saved by not one bell, but two: first the house phone and then the doorbell. The phone stopped ringing abruptly—it must have roused Stacey from her dead-to-the-world slumber—so I excused myself and ran to the front door for the second time that morning.

And, naturally, there was my actual flower delivery.

"No," I told the delivery girl, feeling my stomach churn. "There's been some mistake." *And it's called my life.*

"No mistake," the girl chirped, thrusting the flowers at me. "Bloom, Eighth Street. Sign here, please."

I signed my dignity away, and then reluctantly dragged myself back into the house with my rightful roses.

"*Again?*" Scott cried when I entered the kitchen, which was *so* not part of his script.

Audre, knowing something was seriously off, made a panicked face at me.

"Gosh, *you've* been busy lately, Norah," Francesca commented.

"I'm not saying anything," Neil said.

But the worst was James. He was looking down at the table, looking like he might be fighting back laughter.

For a split second, I saw a way to salvage this debacle—I could simply and sanely tell the group that these flowers were for my sister, and then move ahead with our harmless book talk. After all, I already *had* one bouquet to back me up.

But now, with the second vase of roses in my hand, and the whole group watching me, I felt a tumbling mix of greed and recklessness. If I wanted to go all-out Rosamund, weren't *two* bouquets better than one? The more admirers, the merrier.

Yes. I know. I was diving off the deep end. But I was also hoping—foolishly—that this impromptu change of plans could work in my favor.

"I guess I *have* been busy," I replied, trying to keep my voice steady as I held the vase aloft. "These are from another guy I've been seeing. His name is . . ." I thought fast and desperately. "Lorenzo."

Audre choked on her toast, James coughed, and Neil said, "You actually know someone named *Lorenzo*?"

Did I ever.

Before I could respond, I heard a girl's voice cry out from the living room.

"Where are my *flowers*?" the voice demanded imperiously.

I froze.

As the kitchen door swung open, I turned slowly to see Stacey rushing toward me in her pajamas, eyes sparkling and cheeks pink.

When Stacey and I were younger, we'd pretend we had ESP. We would each close our eyes, try to figure out what the other was thinking (usually, for both of us, it was "I want ice cream") and shriek when we were right. Now I once again tried to send my sister a mental message: *Get out of here. Turn around and walk out and forget about your flowers.*

She didn't hear me.

"Dylan just called," Stacey said, grabbing for the vase in my hand. "He said he sent roses—ooh! They're so pretty."

I jerked back, fear gripping me. "These are—these are mine," I managed to stammer, which was pretty much my first nonlie of the morning.

Stacey stuck her tongue out at me and pointed to the roses on the counter. "Then *those* are mine!"

I heard murmurs from the table. I was reminded of Audre's party and the awful, sinking realization that my scheme was collapsing.

"You're wrong," I told Stacey, backing up. "Those are, um, for me too."

Stacey squinted. My little sister may be a little too into sparkly lip gloss and Jesse McCartney, but she's not stupid.

"Norah," she hissed, slowly walking toward me. "Stop lying. There's no way *you* got two bouquets."

The devil, I realized, does not wear Prada. She wears pink pj's and fluffy *It's Happy Bunny* slippers.

"How do you know?" I snapped. Suddenly, I was sick of always being boy-less and flowerless. The lame Bloom sister. Stacey never saw me any other way—and that was how I saw myself too. It wasn't fair. "Not everything is about *you*, you little brat," I added, gritting my teeth and glaring at my sister.

"Give . . . me . . . *my flowers*!" she

whined, pushing past me toward the counter. "I'm gonna tell Mom!" she added, lunging for the bouquet.

I grabbed Stacey's arm to stop her, but then I realized that the entire book group was about to witness me wrestling with my little sister.

Not the mature and sexy image I'd been going for.

So I gave in, stepping out of her way and shrugging. Stacey promptly scooped up the vase and flounced out of the kitchen, but not before yelling "I hate you!" over her shoulder.

I swallowed the lump in my throat, hoping I wouldn't dig myself in even deeper by bursting into tears. Too bad I couldn't repeat the out-of-body experience from Audre's party. Remembering *that* disaster, I felt another tug of grief. *Strike two.* What was *wrong* with me? Why did Rosamund's risky stunts always run so smoothly, so neatly? And why were *all* of mine flopping?

I turned back to my book group, defeated. There was a long silence as James, Neil, and Francesca gawked at me and Scott and Audre exchanged mournful glances. Nobody was even pretending to look at their copies of *The Devil Wears Prada*. Apparently, my train wreck of an existence was much more interesting than high fashion and the bitchy people who work at magazines.

"That was my sister," I finally said, as if that explained things.

"But why did you let her take the bouquet?" Francesca asked, still looking suspicious.

I sighed and set down my "real" bouquet. A wave of fatigue washed over me. I didn't have the slightest energy to invent another lie.

"It's a long story," I replied with a sigh.

And that, I realized, was *all* it was. A story. Rosamund's story. What had I been *thinking*? I couldn't follow in the footsteps of a *fictional character*. Of course Rosamund's plans ended up successful—she wasn't real! There are no evil little sisters or teasing boys or random mishaps in romance novels. But life is rife with that stuff. Life is not fiction, and fiction is not life, and I needed to stop confusing the two.

Francesca resumed the fascinating *Devil*

discussion ("Let's talk about the use of shoes, okay, guys?") and the rest of the group turned their attention to her. But I dropped my chin in my hands, spacing out and wondering if I should give Rosamund a breather. So far, she'd brought me nothing but humiliation—which I could have achieved fine on my own, without her help. The Rosamund plan had only taken my natural ability to embarrass myself and multiplied it by a thousand. Ever since I'd begun the wild schemes, I'd lost all sense of reason. The only thing *To Catch a Duke* would catch me, it seemed, was a spot in the crazy house.

I studied James across the table—his long-fingered hands, soulful lips, and blue eyes—and, heart aching, accepted that there was no point in pursuing him anymore. I'd tried, and failed. Rosamund and Lorenzo would simply go back under my bed, where they belonged. I'd simply wait for the book group to end, and my crush on James to run its course, kind of like a high fever.

Ten

Spring fever. It usually sets in around May, and this year's case was stronger than ever. Why? Three little letters: SAT.

The exam itself was a hellish Saturday morning full of headaches and hand cramps that I wouldn't wish on my worst enemy. Then a few agonizing weeks later came the tense Wednesday when our scores were posted online.

Clutching hands in the Millay computer lab, Audre and I held our respective breaths as our respective pages loaded. When the scores came up, we both shrieked, but for different reasons. We *both* did better than expected, which was a giant relief for me, but a huge letdown for Audre. As twisted as it sounds, she was literally *hoping* to get a really bad score so she could avoid the whole Yale issue with her parents. Meanwhile, *my* euphoria at scoring higher than a four hundred on the math section lasted until homeroom, when my teacher reminded me that I had my sure-to-be-awful follow-up meeting with Ms. Bliss the next day. I'd written the appointment down on my calendar at home ages ago, but had since pushed the whole thing out of my mind. Somehow, I suspected Ms. Bliss would find a way to shoot down my good score.

Stressed, Audre and I decided to treat ourselves to a movie after school. There was a Japanese film showing at the Angelika, this trendy theater near Millay that's always showing foreign and indie films. Since Scott was out on a blind date with some guy Ha-Jin had set him up with, Audre invited her brother along to fill the "boy" slot. Langston was done with college for the year, and his girlfriend was living in London for the summer, so he was totally available.

Which was a nice treat. Even though Langston is practically the brother I never had, I still think he's drool-worthy, and extremely smart.

While we were sitting in the theater, waiting for the previews to start, I was asking Langston all the college questions I'm usually too timid to ask Griffin.

I was crossing my legs and just getting to "What's your favorite course?" when Audre leaned across Langston to poke me in the arm.

"Could we *not* talk about college for two seconds?" she grumbled. "I swear, I get it enough at home." She pulled her wallet out of her green patent leather hobo bag. "It's always 'Langston takes the best classes at Yale' and 'You know, when *Langston* was a high school junior, he spent twelve hundred and fifty hours on his homework every night.'"

I giggled, because Audre had just done a pitch-perfect imitation of her dad.

Langston laughed too, his big brown eyes twinkling. "Oh, Aud. You know it doesn't make any difference. You're still our parents' favorite."

"Uh-huh," Audre muttered. She jumped up and brushed past us into the aisle. "I'm getting popcorn."

This was a bad sign; Audre usually thinks

movie theater popcorn is junk and only eats it when she's royally pissed. I watched her walk off, and turned back to Langston with a sigh.

"Excuse the sibling rivalry," he said, grinning.

"Please," I said. "I'm an expert." Stacey and I had been avoiding each other ever since our kitchen smackdown in April. My sister was all wrapped up in her gooey reunion with Dylan. And, after putting an end to my Rosamund schemes, I had thrown myself into homework and rereading *Bitter Ironies* for our last session—which was that coming weekend.

"Besides," I added, "Audre's just upset about the SATs and the whole culinary school issue." *And the fact that she hasn't seen Griffin since he left her party with that Eva chick.* I didn't say that, though; Audre hadn't told Langston about her love for Griffin—we keep our boy matters private from him. "It's a hard time for *all* of us juniors," I mused aloud, leaning back in my seat. "Because we know all this change is coming soon."

"You're so insightful, Norah," Langston said, studying me. "I think you're really going places. Audre told me about this book group you started, and it sounds like a success." He patted my arm.

"Going places?" I repeated, blushing a little. I know Langston has a girlfriend and all, but getting attention from a luscious guy like him is still flattering. I didn't have the heart to tell him that the group was anything but a success, so I stalled, feeling the subway rumble beneath my feet. That's one of the cool quirks of the Angelika—it's built right above the Broadway-Lafayette subway station, so the trains roaring underneath you kind of add to the whole moviegoing experience.

I was about to change the subject and ask Langston if he found the subway thing pleasant (as I did) or distracting (as Audre did) when I heard James's voice coming from the back of the theater.

Yes. *James.*

Positive I was losing my mind, I turned in my seat and saw him coming down the aisle. He wore a hoodie under a denim jacket, and his dark hair was rumpled; he looked scrumptiously scruffy.

But James didn't live or go to school in the city—why was he here? Then I noticed the girl at his side, and my heart jumped. Was James on a *date*? The girl looked about fourteen, and she had shoulder-length dark brown hair and big blue eyes.

She was a double of James.

I relaxed. *Of course.* She had to be his *sister*, the one he'd mentioned taking to dance class. And right behind them came a man and woman. The woman had James's blue eyes, and the man his tall, slender frame and dark hair. James's parents. They looked youngish and hip—the dad in a leather jacket, and the mom in a belted denim coat that I completely would have worn. They were probably editors or journalists or, at the very least, people who liked to read novels and *not* science journals. Lucky James. It all made sense now; the fun, smart Roth family was on a movie outing together. I watched the family approach, and then I realized that James would see me at any second. I stiffened.

"Norah, are you okay?" Langston tapped my shoulder. "What are you staring at?"

When I turned back to face Langston, I noticed that he still had one hand on my arm from before. His other hand was now on my shoulder. To someone who didn't know better, it would almost look like he was putting his arms around me. And Audre's seat was still empty. Langston and I could easily have been a couple on a date.

Before I could stop it, my mind leaped to Rosamund, and her impressive step number three: pretending that her handsome brother-in-law, Fitzgerald, was her beau.

"Come now, Fitzgerald," she had whispered, taking his arm as they promenaded past Lorenzo in town. *"Let us pretend we are desperately in love. I will explain all later."* And they had cuddled and kissed and left Lorenzo in a fit of jealous rage. (Fitzgerald, actually, had been *too* happy to comply and tried to *really* seduce Rosamund right afterward. But his wickedness became a separate subplot that ended in his death by drinking and reckless horseback riding.)

I know, I know. I had sworn off Rosamund and her silly stunts. But how perfect was this moment? There I was, with *my* (much nicer) Fitzgerald, while my (much more difficult to get) Lorenzo was only inches away from noticing us. I'd be a moron to let the opportunity pass me by.

And, trust me, if you had your pick of any guy in the world to pose as your fake boyfriend, you'd want Langston.

James and his family were almost across the aisle from us. Time was running out. Still facing Langston, I slipped my arms around his neck and wriggled in closer. I was going places, all right. I tried to drape my leg across his lap but the armrest was in the way so I settled for resting my forehead against his and giving him what I hoped was a seductive smile. I wondered if I should try to kiss him, but that might be pushing it; besides, did I *really* want my first kiss to be with Audre's older brother?

Langston, I should say, tried to bite the heads off my Barbie dolls when I was seven, and used to mock me for wearing headgear retainers when I slept over at Audre's in middle school. That was during what Audre's mom kindly called Langston's "awkward stage," before he'd discovered contact lenses, dreadlocks, and the gym. So Langston and I had just enough history between us to make this moment feel sort of incestuous.

And, from Langston's point of view, totally alarming.

"Norah, what—what are you *doing?*" he spluttered. He pulled back, looking terrified.

Poor Langston. He hadn't been expecting bookish, innocent little Norah to turn all temptress on him.

"Just play along," I whispered, clinging tighter to him. "Pretend we're on a date."

"Norah, you're like a sister to me—I can't—we shouldn't—" Langston rambled on as if he hadn't heard me. "There's Jill, and—"

His girlfriend. How thoughtful. How annoying.

"Fake it," I hissed. James had to be at the row across from us by now. I snuggled in closer. "Please," I added. "I'll explain everything lat—"

Suddenly, I heard chorus of voices in the aisle behind me.

"Norah?" That was James.

"Ew, I *hate* PDA." That sounded like it could be his sister.

"Uh, who wants to explain to me what's going on here?" Definitely Audre. Who did *not* sound happy.

Very slowly, I turned around. James and his sister were standing in the aisle. James was watching me with one eyebrow raised while his sister scowled at us; she probably still hadn't decided if she thought boys were gross or not. James's parents had staked out four seats, but were also glancing over with interest. And, finally, there was Audre, her hands on her hips and her popcorn in a bright yellow heap at her feet.

Not good.

First, I flashed Audre a look that I hoped translated to: *Rosamund! Sorry! Later!*

Then I faced James. "Hi there," I said in my most casual voice. "Meet my boyfriend, Langston."

"Oh, Lord," Audre muttered.

If James was shocked by this introduction, he didn't show it. He simply lifted his chin and stuck out his hand for Langston to shake. "Nice to meet you," he said. I couldn't believe it. James was being polite!

Duh. What had I been thinking? This wasn't *To Catch a Duke*. Even if James was jealous—which he didn't seem to be—he wasn't going to challenge Langston to a duel or anything.

Though that might have been sort of exciting.

"Norah, can you let go of me?" Langston asked quietly. Not usually what boyfriends say. Then I realized I still had my arms wrapped tightly around him, boa-constrictor style. Smooth, right?

I dropped my arms, and Langston returned James's handshake, looking at me like I was a sociopath.

"These are my parents and my sister, Dina," James said as Audre stalked by us to get back to her seat. He turned to his family. "These are some kids from that book group," he explained casually. I felt a small pang of disappointment. I guess I'd been hoping he would say, *This is Norah Bloom— you know, the love of my life?* His parents nodded and smiled but Dina pouted.

"You mean the book group you won't let me join?" she demanded, frowning at James. In bell-bottom jeans, a gasoline attendant shirt, and no makeup, Dina looked much more low-key than Stacey. But I wondered if she and James had some sibling issues of their own.

"We don't read the kind of books *you*

like," James replied, grinning and giving her a nudge.

The lights dimmed then, so James and Dina sat down next to their parents, ending the discussion.

"Norah, you are *unbelievable*," Audre whispered, leaning across Langston to glare at me. "I thought you said you were done with Rosamund. And using my *brother* is just disgusting—"

"I couldn't help it," I whispered, shrugging sheepishly. "Opportunity was, like, kicking down the door. I'm, um, really sorry, Langston." Shame colored my cheeks.

"Oh, it's no problem," Langston lied, moving as far away from me as possible.

"Shhh!" a guy in the back row called. "That's *so* inconsiderate."

"I hate people who talk at movies," a girl agreed loudly.

Audre, Langston, and I all shut up and faced the screen, where some preview or other was blaring. I hoped the two of them could forgive me; Audre would probably get over it soon, but Langston might never want to be alone with me again. I sighed forlornly.

"Hey." A whisper came from across the aisle, and I tensed up. Had my sigh disturbed someone else? I glanced to my right, and in the darkness, I could make out James, also in an aisle seat. He was looking at me, a teasing smile tugging at his lips.

"What about Sebastian?" he whispered.

My heart soared with sudden, unexpected hope. James remembered my fake admirer! He *was* paying attention.

"He's still around," I whispered back, smiling, in the best imitation of Rosamund I could muster.

"Good to know," James whispered. Then he faced forward again.

And, in that moment, I knew what I had to do. I'd come this far in the Rosamund plan—there was no reason not to finish. After all, Rosamund hadn't won Lorenzo until she'd completed big, bad step number four: going after his best friend, Count Alberto.

Now it was my turn.

The minute I got home, before I could lose my nerve, I called Neil.

"Hi, it's Norah," I began, my stomach clenching, and then I stopped, at an utter loss.

How on earth did a girl ask a boy out? I wished I had a handbook or something to check for advice. Then I remembered the line Audre had suggested when we'd been analyzing the James situation back in April.

"I'd really like to get to know you better," I told Neil in a rush.

"You would?" Neil asked, sounding surprised. I heard beeps and booms in the background and realized he was playing a computer game. For some reason, knowing that made me feel less nervous. I was talking to good old *Neil*. I could totally do this.

"Of course," I replied, as if my interest in Neil had been obvious all along. "Maybe, um, we could have dinner somewhere in the neighborhood?" I blurted.

There. Mission accomplished. Asking boys out actually isn't all that hard, once you just make yourself go through with it.

"Oh, I get it," Neil said after a long silence. "This is a trick, right?"

Okay, *now* I was nervous. Was Neil on to me? He *was* supersmart; maybe he'd pieced together exactly what was going on.

"I know how girls work," Neil went on sagely. "You want to get back at me for the secret-admirer note, so you're making me think this is a date and then you'll stand me up to embarrass me." He paused. "Did I figure it out?"

I flopped back against my pillows, relieved. Neil's confusion was almost cute.

"Girls," I replied, "are *not* all about tricks and schemes." I blushed. *Well, except for me and Rosamund.* "Anyway," I continued, "how about this Friday night? I won't stand you up. Honest."

"Friday?" Neil repeated. "Isn't the Philippa Askance reading on Saturday morning?"

Which is perfect, I realized. If Neil and I ran out of stuff to talk about, we could always do last-minute event planning.

But it didn't matter even if the date sucked; the whole point was that Neil would tell James about it, just like Alberto had told Lorenzo. The parallels were so deliciously apparent, I couldn't help but grin to myself.

After a few more awkward stops and

starts, Neil and I finally agreed to meet on Friday night at MeKong, this Vietnamese restaurant in the Slope.

"Hey, Norah?" Neil said before we clicked off, and then he lowered his voice. "I'm really glad you decided to ask me out."

What have I done? I wondered when I clicked off. Now Neil thought I was into him. What if he tried to put the moves on me during our date? I closed my eyes and imagined him leaning forward to kiss me over a bowl of pad Thai. Not that Neil was unattractive, but still—I didn't want to actually make out with him in order to get James. *Ugh.*

When I opened my eyes, I looked across the room at my Magritte calendar hanging on the wall. "Meet with Ms. Bliss—3 p.m. sharp!" I'd scribbled in the slot for Thursday. Tomorrow.

I groaned aloud. Right. Suddenly, the Neil date didn't seem so crucial. First, I had to survive another Bliss attack.

Eleven

"Norah Bloom," Ms. Bliss greeted me when I came into her office the next afternoon. She glanced up from a file on her desk. "Lovely to see you again."

I felt a serious flash of dèja vu as I sank into the chair across from her. This time, I stared down at my silver ballerina flats instead of my orange Pumas, but the fluorescent office lights were still buzzing loudly. Ms. Bliss took a dainty sip from her coffee cup and crossed her long legs. Today, she was busting out of a peach-colored suit but was apparently trying to downplay her Victoria's Secret vibe by wearing wire-rimmed glasses and her hair up in a bun. It wasn't really working.

"So," Ms. Bliss said, riffling through some papers, "it seems you've had a lot going on since February."

Instinctively, I glanced at the wooden frame on her desk, which now held a photo of a blond, muscular guy standing on a dock and holding up a gigantic fish. Definitely not the gym trainer who'd been in that frame on Valentine's Day.

Apparently Ms. Bliss had also had a lot going on since February.

"Mr. Whitmore sent me a very interesting memo," Ms. Bliss was saying.

My English teacher? I glanced at her, worried. Was it about that time he'd caught me and Audre passing notes instead of listening to his mind-numbing lecture on Ralph Waldo Emerson?

"I can explain," I said.

"I see he approved a book group you started," Ms. Bliss went on, still looking at her papers. "Along with Scott Harper and Audre Legrand?" She flashed me her sparkly smile. "Impressive. I met with Audre last month—she's such a poised young lady, wise beyond her years. And Scott—well, he's just one of my favorites."

No surprise that Ms. Bliss would adore Activity Boy. "He's amazing," I agreed, reminding myself to thank Scott and Audre for being my friends, especially after my recent Rosamund insanity.

"Tell me about this book group, Norah," Ms. Bliss said, tapping her Marshmallow nails (it's a curse—having Stacey for a sister, I always recognize nail polish shades) on the desk.

Tell her about the book group? What could I say? *Well, there's this boy I'm in love with but I just asked his best friend out on a date, and there's this bitchy girl with a secret past who might or might not be sleeping with the hot college boy my best friend is in love with, and Scott is taking a break from love, though he did go on a date last night. . . .*

"What sorts of books did you read?" Ms. Bliss prompted.

I blinked. Books. Right. That *was* supposed to be the whole point of the group— not who was in love with whom. How did my little extracurricular club turn into a soap opera?

Coming to, I told Ms. Bliss everything— well, everything that would matter to a college counselor. I told her about *The Curious Incident of the Dog in the Night-Time*, *The Devil Wears Prada*, *Bitter Ironies*, and the upcoming Philippa event we'd organized. As I talked, I started to realize that we *had* kind of done a lot, especially considering half of us had hated each other in the beginning. Maybe the book group *was* an actual accomplishment. Who knew?

Ms. Bliss thought so. "Colleges will love this, Norah," she declared. "And, considering your solid SAT scores and improved midterm grades, I'd say your college future is looking much, much brighter. You might even have a shot at Vassar."

I beamed, wondering if it would be bad form to hug your guidance counselor. Vassar The funny thing was, after starting the book group, I'd become less obsessed with the idea of college. Yes, I'd still browse through different schools' Web sites or, sometimes, when I was fighting my way up a crowded staircase at Millay, I'd imagine I was walking up the massive stone steps of a Gothic library instead. But maybe because the book group, the Philippa hunt, and my pursuit of James had been keeping me so busy, I'd stopped feeling like my real life wouldn't begin until college. The book group had shown me that there was a whole *other* life to be had—even while I was still stuck in high school.

In any case, Ms. Bliss's declaration still made me shiver with anticipation, and I thanked her profusely.

Ms. Bliss nodded, wished me a "productive" summer (standard guidance counselor speak), and promised we'd meet again in the fall.

"Oh, and, Norah?" Ms. Bliss called from her desk. When I turned around, she was smiling.

"I just wanted to say," she added, "that you seem . . . different. You're not the same girl you were in February."

I thought back to that rainy Valentine's Day—back before I'd started the book group, or met James, or read *To Catch a Duke*. I *had* been someone else then, in a way. "Good different or bad different?" I asked warily.

"Good," she answered. "Definitely good." She paused. "I think something great is waiting around the corner for you."

College? I wondered. *Boyfriends?* I had

no idea what she meant. But when I met Audre at the Book Nook that afternoon, I'd have to tell her that Ms. Bliss wasn't that evil after all.

It felt like a tradition—a post-Bliss gossip session in the Book Nook café. Audre and I grabbed a small table by the window and sipped frozen hot chocolates while sneaking peeks at Griffin, who was working behind the register.

After we'd rehashed my recent triumph, Audre shared two crucial pieces of news. The first was that she *hadn't* gotten the summer job at Ozzy's—they'd called her cell that afternoon to say her baking style was too "fancy" for them. The second was that Derek Dawson, her once-scrawny, now sexy, ex had asked her out in gym class.

"What should I do?" she whined, sounding very un-Audre—and very me, actually.

"About Ozzy's? Forget 'em," I replied, stepping into *her* usual decisive role. "You can find something even better. And about Derek?" I grinned. "Go for it. Absolutely."

Audre bent her straw in half, frowning. "Did you notice that this frozen hot chocolate was made with soy milk?" she asked, staring at her drink while I rolled my eyes. "Okay, okay," she said. "Avoiding the subject. I *know* I should say yes to Derek. But . . ." She tilted her head toward the register, where Griffin was working alongside Patrick.

"*Still* holding out hope?" I asked, surprised. "Even after Eva and Francesca?"

Audre nodded firmly. "I'm gonna take your advice, Nors," she whispered. "Well, *my* advice. On Saturday, at our last book group meeting? I'm just going to walk up to him and say, 'I like you. A lot. So now choose: me, Eva, or Francesca.'"

"You can always throw Francesca's physics photo in as an added bonus," I giggled.

"Hey, if it comes to that." Audre finished her drink and sat back. "I figure, what do I have to lose? Our group is ending. If I embarrass myself, I just won't come to the Book Nook ever again. It's like the last day of school—suddenly, everybody gets brave."

I nodded. Saturday *would* be our last session. Who else would be feeling brave that day?

Probably not me.

"Haven't seen you girls in a while," Griffin said, strolling up to our table. I swear I think he listens in on our conversations so he can interrupt whenever we talk about him. "I've been *swamped* with finals and stuff," he added, pulling up a chair. "But I'm finally seeing the light at the end of the tunnel—I'm totally going to party tonight."

"With who?" Audre asked casually, and I knew she was thinking, as I was: *Eva? Francesca? Some random hot girl in your art history class?*

Griffin grinned, his tan fingers playing with his shell necklace. "Just some buddies from my dorm. Anyway, fill me in. What's the book group scoop?"

"Can I tell him?" Audre asked me with a mischievous smile.

"Tell him what?" I was still distracted, thinking about my bravery, or lack thereof.

Audre gave me a *duh* look. "About your *date*." I'd filled Audre in on the Neil portion of the scheme during our subway ride to school that morning.

"Ooh, what date?" Griffin asked, leaning over and jabbing my shoulder, which—surprise—made my face turn red.

"Go for it," I mumbled. My date wasn't really a secret. And maybe the more people who knew about it, the sooner it would get to James.

"It's with Neil," Audre announced. "Tomorrow night. MeKong. Hot stuff, right?" Then she flinched, laughing abruptly, as I threw my straw wrapper at her.

Griffin's *surf's up!* smile faded abruptly and he looked at me. "What's this? *Neil*, from the book group?" He sounded concerned.

Okay, weird. Why did Griffin suddenly care so much about Neil? Or me?

"Are you and him serious?" he was asking. "I mean, I didn't even know you were into each other that way."

We're not, I wanted to say. But Griffin's random interest felt so intense that I could barely speak. I glanced at Audre, who raised her eyebrows and shrugged.

"So . . . speaking of dates, Nors," she said, clearly trying to change the subject, "did you get to talk to Scott during math today?"

I nodded, swallowing a mouthful of frozen hot chocolate. Scott and I are in the same ninth period math class. That's where we usually exchange our crucial information, and one of us fills Audre in later.

"How did his date go?" Audre asked eagerly, leaning forward.

"Scott had a date?" Griffin interrupted. Again, he looked worried. What was his *deal*? He was usually Mr. Mellow—but now he was stressing over the love lives of every book group member?

"Uh . . . yeah," I said. I looked back at Audre, who shrugged again. "Anyway, he said it was a major flop. The guy was completely boring and didn't seem into art or books or movies. They had nothing to talk about."

"Really?" Griffin asked. "So is Scott—"

"Griff! Hey, man, can you cover for me?"

Patrick was calling from the register, where a curvy redhead—probably his girlfriend—stood waiting.

"Oops, gotta go." Griffin got to his feet, all smiles again. "See you ladies this Saturday? Should be good times, providing Ms. Askance shows up."

I nodded, suddenly anxious.

The Book Nook managers sure seemed to think Philippa was showing up. They'd hung a giant poster of her author photo in the window, along with a banner announcing the time of the reading. Stacks of *Bitter Ironies* were on sale at the front of the store, alongside more posters and banners. This was going to the biggest event at the Book Nook—*ever*. And though Philippa's über-helpful agent and editor were handling the nitty-gritty details, I knew it was also up to the book group to make sure things went off without a hitch. Philippa's big appearance had been *our* idea, after all. So, if it didn't work out, we'd be to blame.

But no pressure or anything.

The next night, I was under another kind of pressure. With forty minutes to go until my Neil date, I still hadn't picked my outfit or dried my hair. Instead, I was locked in the steamy bathroom, wrapped in a robe and trying to shave my legs and brush my teeth at the same time (a terrible idea, by the way).

Really, I shouldn't have cared how I

would look for Neil—*he* wasn't the boy I wanted. But Neil was just one step away from James. And if guys—like girls—went over all the details of a date with their friends, I'd want Neil to tell James I'd looked—to quote one of my trial love letters—"smoking." It wasn't like Rosamund had worn a potato sack when she'd gone to a ball with Alberto.

The problem? I was born without that gene that makes most girls good at primping. Makeup and hair products and eyelash curlers are like alien objects to me. So getting myself together takes about five hours longer than it would for any other girl.

Like, say, my sister.

"Norah!" Stacey pounded her little fist on the bathroom door. "You've been in there forever! What's going on?" Usually, *she* was the one taking forever in the bathroom, but I knew she didn't have a date tonight; though Stacey and Dylan were still happily together, she had to stay in and study for a French test.

I hadn't told anyone in my family about my date. Stacey, who I was still pissed at, would only make fun of me. And, knowing my parents, they'd do something totally random, like decide to tag along and wind up chatting with Neil about astrophysics all night.

But as Stacey continued to bang on the door and as I got more and more sweaty and panicked—*Mousse or gel? What's the difference? And why are both those names so scary?*—I realized shutting Stacey out might not be the answer. This once, my shallow sis could actually help, rather than mess things up.

In a time of need, there's usually no one better to turn to than your sister—even if you seriously want to shoot her the *rest* of the time.

So, setting down my toothbrush and razor, I unlocked the door, faced Stacey, and said, "Okay, I have something to tell you, but you have to promise not to: (a) tease me, (b) tell Mom and Dad, or (c) force any of your sequined halter tops on me."

Stacey's face lit up. "It's about a boy, isn't it?"

I felt a twinge of satisfaction. Tonight, I *wasn't* the lame sister! Now that I had a date, my status was magically elevated in my sister's eyes. And, despite myself, I kind of enjoyed that feeling of being admired.

I gave Stacey the two-second rundown on the date (though I did act as if it were real—not part of a plan stolen from a book), and my lack of primping skills—which she knew about already. Stacey nodded wisely.

"You need help," she declared. "Bad."

I shrugged, hating that she was right.

She clapped her hands, all business. "Leave it to me," she announced, and started dragging me out of the bathroom.

"Hang on," I said, remembering how she'd dressed me for Langston's "Come As You Aren't" party. "Can you, uh, make me look like my normal self? You know, no backless dresses or—"

Stacey groaned, cutting me off. "Who's the pro here? You or me?"

She got to work, brushing my hair straight and shiny, glossing my lips berry, and carefully lining my eyes. Then she helped me piece together an outfit—a low-slung denim skirt paired with the faux-diamond-studded belt Ms. Bliss had

mocked back in February, a V-neck raspberry sweater, and my trusty cowboy boots.

"Wow," I said, looking in the mirror. I
did look like myself—only better. "You *are*
a pro."

"You should wear skirts sometimes—
not always jeans," Stacey advised sagely.
"You'll get more boys if you show off your
legs."

Hmm, I thought. Stacey was obviously
doing something right in life—it wasn't
like *she* had to send herself roses to get
some guy's attention. I knew my sister
would inevitably piss me off in the very
near future, but, in that small window of
time during which we'd get along, maybe
I could stand to learn a little bit from her.

As I was heading out the door, suddenly
a bundle of nerves, Stacey crammed a pack
of Orbit gum into my beaded bag.

"Chew two pieces after dinner," she
warned, as a final piece of dating advice.
"Because, chances are, he's going to kiss
you."

Twelve

Stacey's words were echoing in my head—and freaking me out—as I walked into MeKong. The candelit restaurant was crowded, and the spicy scents of peanut sauce and lime drifted in from the back kitchen. Neil was at a corner table, reading the menu. He didn't see me right away, so that gave me a chance to check him out.

My stomach sank; Neil looked good. His wavy black hair was parted on one side and neatly combed. He wore glasses with new, funkier frames, a striped button-down shirt, and khakis. There was no doubt about it: Neil expected action tonight.

Maybe kissing Neil would be a smart

move, I thought. Maybe he'd tell James I was a good kisser—I didn't know if I'd be decent at kissing or not, but really, how hard could it be? Maybe when Neil walked me home, I could even do something bold like reach for his hand or—

Slow down there, Bloom, I thought as Neil caught my eye and waved. We hadn't even *eaten* yet and I was already planning our hook-up?

I started for the seat across from him, but Neil leaped up, walked around the table, and pulled the chair out for me. He semi-bumped into me as he was doing this, so I almost fell, but then he caught my arm and helped me into the chair. I could smell his aftershave—something sharp and spicy. My face was burning. What was with the gentleman stuff? Was this the same *Lord of the Rings*–loving Neil who'd read aloud my letter at Audre's party?

Neil sat back down and smiled at me across the table. "I took the liberty of ordering for you," he said, as if he always talked this way. "I hope it's to your liking."

Oh-kay. Neil was suddenly acting like . . . a player.

"I guess it depends what you ordered," I said, folding my hands on the table. Right. We were about to eat an entire meal. God, dinner is *long*. And dating is a lot of work. It wasn't fair; Rosamund always seemed to have *fun* with her charades. And mine were anything but fun—unless you considered constant humiliation entertaining.

"Tofu," Neil said, and now I noticed that it wasn't just his choice of words that was unusual. He was also speaking in a strange, low voice that sounded nothing like his normal self. "Didn't you say you were a vegetarian at our last meeting when you were telling the Philippa story?" He winked at me. "I am too."

The thing about winking is this: Only Griffin can get away with doing it and still look cool. Everybody else looks stupid.

"You know," Neil said slowly. If he kept talking in that deep voice, I was going to have to crawl under the table to laugh. "All this time we were in the book group together, I had no clue that you had a crush on me."

So *that* was why he was being—or trying to be—Mr. Suave. It was what I'd suspected when we'd gotten off the phone on Wednesday: Neil was now convinced I was in love with him.

Our food came then, which saved me from having to respond. I wished the waiter would stay forever as he set down our steaming plates. But, of course, he left swiftly and I was alone with Neil again.

And then Neil was doing something else very surprising. Only not that gentlemanly. He was reaching across the table with his chopsticks and plucking a piece of broccoli right off my plate.

"Thanks," he said, grinning.

Uh . . . *no*, thanks. Audre and I eat off each other's plates all the time, which is no big deal when it's your best girlfriend—but on a first date? It's like pretending the two of you are all close and intimate when, in reality, you've kind of just met.

That was when I decided: My first-ever date might have to be my last.

"When you called me on Wednesday," Neil went on, digging into his pad Thai, "everything from the past four months added up."

It did?

"The way you're always looking at me during our meetings—"

I'm looking at James, who always sits next to you!

"And how embarrassed you were when I read that note at Audre's party—"

Well, let's see. Would you like to be publicly humiliated in front of everyone you know?

I was biting both my upper and lower lip to keep from cracking up. "Norah?" Neil asked. "Are you choking or something?" I shook my head, grabbing my water glass and drinking fast to pound back the giggles.

"Once I'd figured all that out, I called James," Neil added.

Now I *was* choking. I put down my water and coughed. "Really? Why?"

"Well . . ." Neil poked his chopsticks into my plate again, but this time I didn't care. "For some reason, I always thought he was into you. He kept saying he liked a girl in the book group but wouldn't tell me who—he's a private guy like that. I guess I wanted to—I don't know—make sure he was okay with our going on a date."

I tried not to gasp. James liked someone

in the book group? "So was he . . . okay with it?" I whispered.

Neil shrugged. "Sure, yeah. He didn't say much. I guess the girl he likes is maybe Francesca or Audre. So we're cool."

We're cool.

The pain felt hot and instant, like I'd slapped my hand on a lit stove. It was over. James didn't like me. *Thanks for nothing, Rosamund.* Abruptly, I realized that there was no point in being on this date anymore. I'd feel bad ditching Neil in the middle of dinner, but sobbing in public would feel much worse.

"I have a migraine—," I started to say, my throat closing with tears, when the restaurant's front door banged open and a gust of warm wind blew in. I glanced over to the door, forgetting my misery for a moment as a wave of shock hit me. The girl striding into MeKong was so unexpected that I was certain I was imagining things. I watched, numb with disbelief as she posed, hand on hip, just as she'd done when I'd seen her for the first time—back in the Book Nook. Then she shook back her glossy black hair and focused her gray eyes right on me and Neil.

"Hi," Francesca Cantone spoke across the restaurant.

Excuse me?

I turned to Neil in confusion, but he shook his head, just as clueless.

Francesca click-clacked toward us in her skinny heels, brushing by a waiter and ignoring the stares of the other diners. Her face was flushed and her jaw was set.

Why was she *here?*

She stopped by our table and looked at me coldly. "Am I interrupting your time together?" she snapped.

Whoa—Francesca's bitchiness was out full force. I racked my brain, wondering if I'd done something to upset her at our last meeting. I hadn't made too much fun of *The Devil Wears Prada*, had I?

"Well," Neil was saying, "we *are* on a date. . . ."

"No," I jumped in. "It's okay." Maybe I could use Francesca's mysterious appearance as an excuse to escape. I started to push back my chair.

Francesca crossed her arms over her chest. Her face was turning pinker by the minute. "Well, are you or aren't you on a date? Are you guys, like, serious now?"

I paused: Those were the exact words Griffin had used, yesterday in the Book Nook.

"Did Griffin tell you we were going to be here?" I blurted. That was the only reason I could think of that she even knew about our "date."

Francesca took a deep breath, and nodded. "He called me last night," she said softly.

"Why?" Neil and I asked at the same time.

Francesca lifted her bare shoulders— believe it or not, she was wearing a tube top, even though it was still coolish outside. "Because he knew," she murmured.

"Knew what?" That was me and Neil again, doing our "in unison" act. This was feeling more and more surreal.

Very slowly, Francesca turned to Neil, and my mouth dropped opened in shock as I identified the expression in her eyes: longing and . . . desire.

"How I felt about you," Francesca whispered.

To *Neil*!

I was dying. I wondered if I could reach into my bag for my cell phone and call Audre without their noticing.

"What are you—talking about?" Neil sputtered, looking stunned. He probably figured one girl (i.e., *me*) liking him was doable. But two at once? And Francesca, no less?

Francesca turned to the bug-eyed couple at the table beside us—they'd obviously been listening to every word—and asked to borrow their extra chair. Then she moved the chair up to our table, next to Neil, and sat down, acting as if this was a perfectly normal setup. We could have been three friends from a book group having a casual dinner together. The waiter even came by to ask Francesca if she wanted a menu, but she waved him off.

"I have something to ask you," she said to Neil, taking another big breath. Her hands were clasped in her lap and I noticed she was trembling. I wondered if I should excuse myself to give them privacy, but this moment was way too delicious/scary to miss.

"Do you remember going to an awards

ceremony at Columbia last year?" Francesca asked quietly.

Oh, yeah! The photo! I nodded eagerly, but neither of them looked at me.

"The City-Wide Physics Contest, sure." Neil frowned. "How did you know I was—"

"There?" Francesca cut in, smiling. "I was there too, Neil. We sat next to each other at the winners' dinner, and we talked about our favorite science-fiction writers the whole time. Remember?" She briefly stared off into the distance, her gray eyes dreamy.

Neil reacted like someone had dumped a tub of ice water on his head. He blinked and shook his head at least five times.

"That was . . . *you?*" he whispered.

You do *like science fiction!* I wanted to cry.

Francesca smirked. "I've improved, huh?"

Neil's face colored. "You weren't too bad. . . ." He must have been remembering those eyebrows.

Francesca laughed. "That's sweet of you, Neil," she said. "But I *was* pretty bad. I didn't know the first thing about clothes. All I lived for was school, and science stuff.

And for fun, my friends and I did"—she shuddered—"Dungeons and Dragons." She whispered this last part as if it were a terrible, evil secret. For the life of me, I couldn't picture Francesca Cantone playing Dungeons and Dragons. "But the night I met you," Francesca went on, her face lighting up, "I realized I needed to change myself. I was so into you, but I knew you didn't like me back. No guys ever did."

I swallowed, suddenly feeling weepy. Who'd ever have thought I'd understand Francesca?

She kept going, her voice determined. "I decided to"—she gestured to her clingy striped tube top, gold nameplate necklace, and Lucky jeans—"fix myself up. Change my style, or whatever. I started to do it in little ways—like, getting contacts, kind of avoiding my friends." She looked so guilty for a moment that I almost wanted to reach over and give her a hug. "Over summer vacation, I went for it big-time: I bought a whole new wardrobe, changed my hair, and even practiced how to *act* different. That was when I made friends with Mimi—she lives in my apartment building, and she noticed my new look, so we started hanging out together." Francesca sighed. "When senior year started in September, I was suddenly, like, *in* Mimi's crowd. I was a new person. I was . . . me." Francesca grew quiet and I could see the relief on her face. She seemed much freer—more relaxed —now that she'd finally uncorked all her long-held secrets.

And now *I* couldn't hold back my innermost thoughts anymore. "So do you really like to read *The A-List* and all that stuff, or was that just made up?" I asked. (For me, it always comes back to books.)

Francesca glanced at me like she'd forgotten I was there. "Oh. Yeah. I'd never read that stuff in my life. Mimi told me about it. I wanted everything I did to match my new . . . image, or whatever." Then she faced Neil, her eyes very big and hopeful. "I wanted to be this . . . this perfect girl you'd fall for when I saw you again."

"When you saw me again?" Neil repeated. He knitted his eyebrows together. "You knew I was going to be in this book group? Or was that just a coincidence?"

Francesca smiled sheepishly. "There's

no such thing as a coincidence," she murmured. "*I* made sure you joined the group, Neil. When Griffin told me about a high school book group that was starting up in Park Slope, I thought of you right away. So I drafted a fake flyer about a sci-fi club—I knew you wouldn't turn that down."

Okay, I realized. *She's insane.*

"*You* mailed that flyer to my house?" Neil could barely get the words out.

Francesca nodded. "I had your address from the contest. I'm sorry, Neil. I know that basically makes me a stalker—"

Neil shook his head. "This is a joke, right? Girls always do stuff like this, don't they?" He was back on his paranoia kick. "You're going to, like, embarrass me in two seconds." He glanced toward the door, as if he expected to see Ashton Kutcher and the whole *Punk'd* crew storming in.

"I swear it's not a joke," Francesca said softly. She reached for Neil's hand. "I thought you even knew by now—I was always trying to flirt with you, get you to pay attention to me. I kept just waiting and hoping you would ask me out. But when Griffin told me about your date with

Norah—" She tipped her head toward me. "I knew I had to *do* something."

I shook my head in awe. As Neil himself had put it earlier, everything was adding up. Neil thinking our group was a sci-fi club that first day. Francesca leaving the Philippa Askance search when James told her Neil wouldn't be there. Francesca cozying up to Neil at Audre's party. And Griffin's unnatural interest in my date tonight.

"So you're *not* with Griffin?" I asked Francesca.

Francesca shook her head, laughing. "Griffin? Not at all. We're just good friends—he's one of the few people that knows about my . . . past. We kind of bonded as soon as we met, so I felt like I could trust him."

"So is he with that girl Eva, then?" I pressed on, knowing Audre would want me to find out for sure.

Francesca giggled. "No way. She's not his type. Neither am I. Lately, he's totally been into—"

"Francesca?" Neil interrupted. He was staring at her. "I, um, still can't believe you would do all that for me." He cleared his throat. "But, okay, if this all for real, can I just say something?" Francesca and I both nodded, and Neil's expression turned serious. "I wish you didn't feel like you *had* to change yourself," he said quietly, sounding more mature than I'd ever heard him. "At that dinner, I literally thought you were the coolest girl I'd ever met—we had so much in common. To be honest, half the time guys don't even notice what a girl is wearing or what her hair looks like." He shrugged. "At least, *I* didn't then. I just noticed . . . you."

Francesca swallowed hard, clearly trying not to cry. I was kind of close to tears myself.

"God, that's so romantic, I'm going to bawl!" the woman at the next table whispered to her boyfriend.

"But don't get me wrong," Neil went on, a grin spreading over his face. "I like you this way, too."

"You do?" Francesca asked, her lower lip trembling, and I saw a glimpse of the awkward girl she had once been.

Neil nodded, and moved his chair

closer so he could put his arm around her. Francesca's face brightened, and then she dropped her head onto his shoulder. Neil gave her a hesitant kiss on the cheek, and she sighed with happiness.

In the weirdest, most *who would have ever guessed it?* way, Francesca Cantone and Neil Singh were . . . cute together. They made sense.

Francesca *wasn't* insane, I realized. She was just in love. And people will do completely crazy things for love—myself included, of course.

Suddenly, I felt wrong being there with the two of them. I stood quickly, pulling my wallet out of my bag. "Uh, guys?" I said. "I'm just gonna, you know, go. . . ."

Neil looked at me, his eyes widening. "Oh, Norah," he gasped. "Right. Um, listen. I'm so sorry about this—I like you and all, but—"

I held up my hand. "Neil. Don't worry. I'm not heartbroken."

Francesca didn't pay any attention to me; she was too busy nuzzling Neil's neck. She sure moved fast. So maybe Neil *would* get action tonight, after all.

I put some money on the table, and, as I hurried away, I saw the woman at the table next to us blowing her nose as her boyfriend patted her arm.

Without warning, I felt a little like crying myself. Not because Francesca and Neil's surprise reunion was choking me up, but because of what Neil had told me *before* Francesca's grand entrance: that James liked someone in the book group—but not me.

Which meant that now I'd never be able to rest my head on James's shoulder, the way Francesca had done so easily with Neil. And though I'd told Neil otherwise, that realization *did* sort of break my heart.

Thirteen

Ring. Ring.

I grabbed for my cell phone, my eyes still half-shut.

"Audre?" I mumbled. "Didn't we just talk, like, two hours ago?"

When I'd returned home the night before, the first thing I'd done was call Audre. We spent hours analyzing the entire surreal date, from Neil's sketchiness to Francesca's shocking confession to Griffin's being "totally into" someone mysterious—who we could only hope was Audre herself. But I *didn't* say anything about James also liking someone else—the possibility that James and Audre might end up together was too bizarre and painful to consider.

When Audre and I finally clicked off near morning, I'd semi-dozed, dreaming restlessly about tofu and physics. Now that it was morning, my head was throbbing.

"It's not Audre," a male voice said. There was a pause. "It's James."

Oh.

"James?" I said, struggling to sit up. James Roth? I looked at my bedside clock, wondering if I'd overslept and missed the reading. It *was* kind of late—I had only fifteen minutes to shower and change—but there was still time. I figured James was calling with some emergency question.

And it was weird, but now that I knew that I had no chance with James, I felt surprisingly calm. Maybe I *was* finally over him.

"I'm glad you called," I said, swinging my legs off the bed and stretching. "I need to get ready for Philippa. Are you at the Book Nook now?"

"No," James replied distractedly. "I'm still at home. So, how was your date?"

I paused, the phone tucked against my ear. "With Neil?"

"Yeah." James swallowed. "He told me that you asked him out."

"I know," I said, my pulse speeding up. "He told me he told you."

"He did?" James was quiet for a second and I pictured him, pacing in his room, like I was pacing now. His voice sounded kind of tense, but I figured that had to do with the Philippa reading. "Well . . . how did it go? Are you guys . . . a couple?"

I started laughing. "Wait—you didn't talk to Neil this morning? You don't know about Francesca?"

"*Francesca?*" James repeated, sounding rattled. "What do you mean?"

"Norah!" Stacey yelled from the hall. "I'm about to get in the shower! Do you need to use the bathroom?" After our bonding last night, my usually selfish sis was still in considerate mode.

"Oh, God," I said to James, looking at the time again. There were now only ten minutes left before we had to be at the Book Nook. "I should go. We both should—we're gonna be late to the Philippa reading!" Then I clicked off and sprinted out into the hall to stop Stacey. I had a reading *and* the last session of my book group to attend. I didn't have time now to ponder the meaning behind James's odd phone call.

I ran into the Book Nook, out of breath, tripping over one of the store cats. My hair was still wet and I was wearing the denim skirt from last night paired with my old Belle & Sebastian T-shirt—the first things I could grab off my floor.

The place was mobbed. It seemed that all of Park Slope had turned out. Endless rows of chairs—each one filled—stretched out in front of the podium near the door. One entire row was filled with people carrying cameras and notepads and wearing official-looking badges around their necks—probably reporters or journalists. A friendly-looking fortyish woman with shaggy-chic blond hair—whom I guessed was Philippa's editor—was helping Patrick stack signed copies of *Bitter Ironies* on a counter. This was *huge*.

I noticed a group of Griffin's NYU buddies, Eva among them, clustered in one corner, but I couldn't find Griffin himself.

Then I saw Audre holding court at a table near the back, proudly passing around slices of the "bitter" lemon pie she'd baked for the occasion. (She'd finished the pie last night during our phone marathon.) The rest of our book group was sitting in the front row seats Griffin had reserved for us; Scott and James (he'd beaten me there!) were comparing their copies of *Bitter Ironies* while Francesca and Neil held hands and stared at each other lovingly.

Suddenly Griffin jogged up to me, out of breath. "Dude, thank God you're here," he said. His blond hair was sticking out all over the place and he looked, possibly for the first time in his life, stressed. "Philippa hasn't shown yet."

"She *hasn't*?" I felt a prickle of panic. "Isn't the reading supposed to start, like, *now*?" The plan was that Philippa would sweep in, do the reading, and then join us in the back for the book group meeting.

Griffin nodded. "Her agent has been calling her every two seconds, but she's not having any luck." He groaned. "If this reading doesn't happen, my boss is going to eat me for brunch." He glanced over his shoulder at the fidgety audience. "And the natives are getting restless," he added. "You know, the editor of *Teen Vogue* is here."

"Crap," I muttered. Had Philippa actually bailed? After our conversation on Seventh Avenue, I'd somehow believed she really was coming. Was that insanely naive of me? "What are we going to do?" I groaned.

"You mean," Griffin corrected, "what are *you* going to do." He put his hands on my shoulders—I forgot to blush—and grinned at me. "You need to say something to the crowd, Norah, just to distract them. At least until Philippa gets here. *If* she gets here."

My skin turning cold, I glanced at the empty podium. Do I even need to tell you that I have horrible stage fright?

"Please," Griffin said, all but pulling me toward the podium. "It'll be fine. You just have to be, like, 'Hi, I'm Norah Bloom, and welcome to this glorious event.' Then just say a few words about why you like to read Philippa's stuff and hope like hell that she walks in the door. You can do it, Norah. You're the leader of this book group, after all."

"I am?" I whispered, my feet stuck to the floor. One of the cats—I think it was Virginia Woolf—rubbed against my legs, as if to remind me: *Yeah, you are, idiot.*

Somehow, with Griffin steering me, I made it to the podium and faced the noisy crowd, trying not to think about the *Teen Vogue* person, or the fact that Philippa's important agent and editor were out there. My legs felt wobbly. I didn't think fainting would even be all that bad in that moment—at least it would take me away for a little while, like a nice vacation.

When I glanced at the front row, where Audre and the rest of the book group sat, I saw them smiling and waving at me. It was kind of calming to know I had their support, though Scott giving me the thumbs-up was making me even more anxious. Then I looked at James. He was watching me, his blue eyes warm and thoughtful, and suddenly, I felt safe. Like I couldn't mess up if James was out there.

"Hi," I spoke into the microphone. The sound of my own voice boomed in my ears, loud and crackly—*ugh*. But I kept going. "I'm Norah Bloom, and I'd like to welcome everyone to this glorious event." A few people laughed, but not in a teasing way. *Say a few words about why you like to read Philippa's stuff,* Griffin had said. "Reading Philippa Askance is . . ." What could I say? I remembered meeting the author on Seventh Avenue, and how easily we'd been able to talk.

"Like hanging out with a friend," I finished. "A really smart, cool friend you wish you could take with you everywhere. And I feel like that's what the best writers *should* be to their readers—friends. People you can rely on and come back to again and again."

That was even true about Irene O'Dell, I realized—*and* my real-life friends. I smiled at Audre and Scott, feeling the tiniest bit choked up. "By now, it's almost like Philippa Askance is a member of our book group," I added on a whim. "We talk about her enough. And"—I was remembering how I'd almost ended the group before we decided to take on the Philippa mission—"we'd probably have broken up a long time ago if it wasn't for her." Everyone laughed again.

"Go, Norah!" Scott whooped. I'd have to yell at him for that afterward.

I was wondering how to wrap things up when the door to the Book Nook opened. Relieved, I turned, expecting to see Philippa in all her punky, bleached-hair glory.

But it wasn't Philippa at the door. It was a tall, skinny teenage bike messenger holding a padded envelope. Griffin hurried over to attend to him, but I listened to their exchange.

"This is kind of weird," the bike messenger said, his eyes darting around the store, "but Philippa Askance asked me to deliver this to"—he looked at what was written on the back of the envelope—"'The Girl from the Book Group with the Long Dark Hair and Dark Eyes who followed me and quoted *Bitter Ironies*,'" he read out loud, then let out a breath and glanced up in confusion. "Is there anyone here who thinks that's supposed to be them?"

I swallowed hard. That was supposed to be *me*.

"That's got to be Norah," Griffin said with a grin—clearly, he'd been filled in on my Philippa stalkage by possibly Francesca. He signed for the package and walked it to me.

My pulse was racing as I stood at the podium and tore open the envelope. I could feel the whole crowd watching me, holding their collective breath.

Inside the envelope was a thick stack of typed pages, and on top of that, a typed letter:

Dear girl who followed me,

As you've probably guessed by now, I won't be coming to the reading today. In the end, it's just not my style. But it's also not my style to blow off a devoted reader who understands all about being better one-on-one. So, enclosed, you'll find the manuscript for my second novel. It will be in bookstores exactly a year from now. Besides my agent and my editor, no one has seen this manuscript yet. I ask that you please not read this out loud at the Book Nook. I'd rather you just read it alone—or share it with other members of your book group if you'd like.

I'm calling the novel Innocent Abandon. *It's a love story.*

Your friend,
Philippa Askance

I read the letter a couple times more, to be sure I wasn't dreaming. The fact that

Philippa wasn't coming today suddenly meant nothing. I had this note—and the knowledge that I'd inspired her second book. What more could I ask for?

I looked up, and spoke into the microphone again. "Philippa Askance can't make it today," I said, hugging the secret manuscript to my chest.

"No way!" a guy hollered from the middle row.

"I demand a refund!" a girl screeched, even though the reading had been free.

"But didn't she *promise*?" I heard Audre ask from the front row.

I grinned, feeling immune to all the chaos. What was it Philippa had told me? *I'll be there in some form. I promise.* And she'd certainly made good on her word.

After Philippa's agent and editor had replaced me at the podium to do some damage control—and hand out the pre-signed copies of *Bitter Ironies*—the store finally cleared out.

When my book group gathered at a table in the café to unwind, and I told everyone about the manuscript. Of course,

I kept parts of the letter—and the story behind the title—to myself. But I promised to make copies for everyone—as long as *they* promised to keep the new novel under wraps until it came out in bookstores next year. Though we were all kind of drained from the morning's events, everyone was totally blown away by the news. The general consensus, as Griffin thoughtfully brought a tray of iced drinks to the table, was: It sucked that Philippa had blown off the reading, but her giving us a sneak peek at the new manuscript was pretty tremendous.

"It's all thanks to Norah," a suddenly angelic Francesca declared. She was sitting in Neil's lap—a sight that would still take some getting used to.

"Who also happened to make a great speech today," Audre added, leaning over to give me a kiss on the cheek. All the embarrassment I'd managed to fight off during that speech rushed to my face on the form of a major blush.

"Here's to Norah!" Scott exclaimed, and everyone toasted with their iced mochas.

"You guys, we did it as a *group*," I insisted,

hating the whole center-of-attention thing. "And, speaking of which, do we still want to have our last group meeting today?" I waved my copy of *Bitter Ironies*.

James looked out the window, shielding his eyes from the bright May sun. "On one condition," he said, and turned back to the group with a smile. "We hold it outside."

"In Prospect Park!" Neil nodded, wrapping his arms around Francesca's waist. "Let's do it!"

"Pretty please, teacher Bloom?" Audre teased.

"Of course," I said, getting to my feet, pleased by the idea of an outside meeting. "It's practically summer."

Francesca, Neil, and James were all quick to gather their stuff, and the three of them started heading toward the front of the store.

"Wanna come with us?" Scott asked Griffin, who was still hovering by the table, and still looking semi-stressed.

Griffin smiled ruefully. "I wish. I've got to work for a couple more hours, at least." And then, unexpectedly, he reached over and touched Scott's shoulder. "I don't want to keep you here now," he added. "But maybe we could hang out some other time?"

Excuse me? I glanced over sharply.

"Just the two of us?" Scott asked, looking as shocked as I felt. I turned to Audre, who had gone rigid and was staring at Griffin in bewilderment.

Griffin nodded, grinning at Scott. "I'll have more free time this summer, since I'm not taking any classes. Maybe we could go to a movie or an art exhibit or something."

Audre finally returned my gaze, her eyes enormous. I knew we were both thinking the same thing:

Griffin is asking out Scott!

"Give me one second?" Scott said after a long pause. He took Audre's arm. "Hey, Aud, um, can you come to the bathroom with me? I'm having contact problems again, and you know how you're good with that stuff."

Just a newsflash: Scott has 20/20 vision, and Audre gets completely grossed out by anything involving eyes.

But, luckily, Griffin didn't know that.

While they were gone, I went over the past several months in my head, just as I had last night after Francesca's confession.

Again, things fell into place once I really thought about them: Griffin coming to Audre's party because he "couldn't pass up this chance to see"—Scott. And he'd even left the party when he found out Scott wasn't there! It also explained why Griffin had been so curious about Scott's blind date yesterday. But was Griffin gay? I remembered Francesca saying she and Eva weren't Griffin's type. At the time, I'd figured she'd been talking about looks or personality. But maybe she'd meant that Griffin wasn't into *girls* at all—which was certainly unexpected. I'd definitely need to find out more, from either Scott, or, if possible, Francesca.

Scott and Audre reappeared; to my relief, neither one of them was crying or bearing any bruises. They looked . . . chill. It was obvious (well, to me) that they'd had a quickie heart-to-heart about Scott dating Griffin. Audre still seemed sort of unsteady on her feet, but she also looked resigned. I knew my BFF had told Scott she was cool with it—even if she wasn't quite yet. But, knowing Audre, she'd move on somehow. She nodded at me, and I nodded back, understanding. We'd talk later.

Scott, meanwhile, was chatting easily with Griffin, saying he'd stick around until the end of Griffin's shift that day. I wondered if Scott might not have suspected the truth about Griffin all along but had ignored his suspicion, sticking to his break-from-love plan. Though I was feeling Audre's pain, part of me was cheering for Scott; after Chad, he deserved a sweetie like Griffin in his life.

Francesca, Neil, and James were already standing by the door, so I linked my arm through Aud's. We were turning to leave when Griffin called out to her.

"Dude, your lemon pie was the hit of the reading," he said. "Well, the nonreading. Even the *Teen Vogue* editor asked about it."

Audre smiled with her lips closed. I knew she was still a little hurt, even if she wanted to accept the compliment. I squeezed her elbow for support.

"Anyway," Griffin went on, "I have this great idea—something I've been thinking about for the past few months. How would you feel about being the snazzy new baker for the Book Nook café? We don't sell pastries right now, but my boss has been thinking about changing that. And I told him I know the perfect person for the job." Griffin pointed at Audre, beaming.

Audre blinked. "Me?" Her dimples were starting to show. It's sort of hard to stay mad—even at the boy who's blown you off for your gay best friend—when you get an offer like that.

"It can just be a summer gig, for now," Griffin went on. "But if your stuff sells well, we could probably offer you a part-time position when school starts." He paused, and gave Audre another one of his slow grins. "Whaddya think?"

Audre glanced at me, her eyebrows raised. She hadn't miraculously recovered from the Griffin-and-Scott shock, but her face was slowly starting to glow, her dimples about to emerge full force. And why not? Getting a chance to create her own edible masterpieces for the Book Nook was ten times better than an assistant position at Ozzy's. And best of all, this opportunity might finally prove to Audre's parents that her baking might lead to a real career (or at least show them how serious she was about trying).

Plus, I realized with a shiver of gladness, Audre might feel boyless now, but there was always Derek Dawson waiting in the wings. . . .

I took her hand and squeezed it hard to show her I thought Griffin's suggestion was the best plan ever.

Audre finally smiled fully at Griffin and nodded. "You're on," she said simply.

Scott looked relieved to see Aud happy, and blew her—and then me—a quick kiss.

Griffin slipped an arm around her shoulder, and Audre stiffened just a bit. But when he told her that his boss wanted to meet with her that very day to discuss the details, Audre was all smiles again.

"I'm sorry, Nors," she said, giving me a hug good-bye. "I'm going to have to skip out on *Bitter Ironies* for this. Enjoy the last meeting of the Brooklyn book group, okay?"

The last meeting. It seemed so final. And with Audre and Scott busy in the Book Nook, it would just be me, Francesca, Neil, and James. I had no idea how the four of us, on our own, would get along. But I hurried to the front of the store, where the others were waiting, to find out.

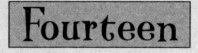

Fourteen

Francesca and I fell into step ahead of the boys, leading the way toward the park. Despite her ten-inch cork-soled sandals and tiny tennis skirt, Francesca seemed more laid-back than I'd ever seen her—she wasn't even wearing makeup. I wondered if now that she was with Neil, she'd slowly morph back into her old self. Or, even better, maybe she'd work out a happy balance between Physics Girl and Wannabe Plum. Either way, I noticed that walking next to her felt surprisingly comfortable; once she'd stopped giving off those hostile, secretive vibes, Francesca Cantone was semicool.

As we crossed Seventh Avenue, Francesca told me she'd be working in a research lab during the summer (which was obviously why she hadn't told us her summer plans back in April) before packing up for Dartmouth in the fall. New Hampshire is pretty close to New York; I kind of hoped that when Francesca came back to the city—as she surely would—to visit Neil, the two of us could meet for coffee sometime.

And now that the Griffin mystery was cleared up, she and Audre might even have a shot at being friends.

"I don't get it," I said then, as we headed up Eighth Avenue toward the park entrance. "So Griffin's *not* straight? He's always so touchy-feely with girls—you, me, Audre, that girl Eva. . . . And I've noticed him checking out different girls in the Book Nook."

Francesca shook her head, laughing. "Oh, Griffin is just . . . Griffin. He likes girls *and* boys. Totally bi-curious. He told me that the first time I met him, at that Guggenheim exhibit in the fall. He was actually there with some random guy he was going out with at the time, and I bumped into them and we all started talking. I think Griffin's doing the whole I'm-in-college-and-I'll-experiment thing, so who *knows* what sexual preference he'll eventually decide on."

"I guess we'll find out someday," I said, shrugging. *Hmm.* That was a side to college I hadn't ever thought about.

When we reached the park, our foursome staked out a shady spot on a grassy hill. Neil, still getting his gentleman on, spread his jacket on the ground for Francesca. James didn't offer to sacrifice his gray cotton hoodie for me, but it was fine—I didn't mind sitting my butt on the warm grass. I let the sun toast my hair, and I closed my eyes. I felt deliciously lazy in an end-of-the-year way, but I still wanted to get into *Bitter Ironies*.

Francesca and Neil, though, wanted to get into something else.

Before I'd even opened the book, Neil had slipped his arm around Francesca's waist and she'd wriggled back into his lap—clearly, her new favorite spot. Rolling my eyes, I asked that classic book group question—what people's favorite part of the story was—but got no responses. When James started to answer me, I couldn't even pay attention to him because Francesca and Neil now had their hands all over each other, kissing and whispering, "That feels so good, baby." I wanted to puke.

Talk about bitter ironies. Neil and Francesca, who I'd never have guessed could work as a couple, suddenly couldn't keep their hands off each other. Meanwhile, James and I, who I'd been imagining as a couple forever, had about a mile of grass between us and could barely look at each other.

Take my word for it: Watching two people seriously make out while your crush is sitting nearby ranks very high on the list of Life's Most Awkward Moments.

"Does *anybody* want to discuss the book?" I finally asked as Francesca and Neil tumbled over onto Neil's jacket, panting.

James cleared his throat. "I do," he said. Then, glancing at Neil and Francesca's makeout marathon, he added, "But can we walk and talk at the same time?"

I was relieved we were on the same page. "Definitely," I said, jumping up just as James leapt to his feet. We waved good-bye to Neil and Francesca, who, needless to say, didn't notice us at all.

James and I half-walked, half-ran away from them, our elbows bumping as we hurried down the hill. When we got to the bottom, we looked at each other and burst out laughing.

"Think they'll ever come up for air?" James asked, his eyes dancing.

"Hmm. Maybe in November?" I giggled.

"I feel bad for all the other people in the park. There are *kids* around here."

On cue, a little boy and girl holding ice-cream cones ran up the hill, right toward where Francesca and Neil were hooking up.

I grinned at James. "We should've warned them, huh?"

James tilted his head to the side, looking mischievous. "They have to find out about that stuff someday, I guess."

We were still laughing as we wandered down one of the emptier park paths. Though I was having fun mocking Francesca and Neil's, uh, enthusiasm for each other, a tiny part of me felt grateful toward them both. If it weren't for Francesca luring Neil to the book group, James would never have joined either. And today, Francesca and Neil had once again inadvertently brought me and James together.

We talked about *Bitter Ironies*, weaving on and off of paths and into the Botanic Gardens. Our conversation—as natural and fluid as water—reminded me of the night we'd talked at Art House. And the setting—the sun-splashed afternoon and the blooming flowers—reminded me of our Philippa search around Park Slope. It was like all my best James memories wrapped into one. After being so tense around James for so long, it felt like sweet relief to just let loose and joke around with him. I wasn't nervous or distracted by my Rosamund schemes anymore. I could just *be*.

We took a break on a wrought-iron bench in a more secluded spot of the park. Low-hanging, leafy-green branches covered us, so I felt hidden from the rest of the world. James and I kept talking, and our conversation shifted from books to movies to our families to school and, somehow, back to Neil and Francesca.

"So that's what you meant this morning, when you asked me if I knew about

Francesca," James was saying. "Neil hadn't called this morning, so I got him to fill me in a little, right before the reading. It kind of makes more sense now, but I still can't get my mind around the two of them together."

"Me neither," I laughed. "And I was there at the start!" Then I told James about Francesca showing up at MeKong.

James studied his hands. "You must have been pretty upset," he said carefully. Then he lifted his head and fixed his light blue eyes on me. "I mean, because you like Neil. Right?"

Was *that* why James had called that morning? To find out if I really did like Neil? Suddenly, my heart was racing, as if it suddenly sensed—independently of me—that the talk was veering in a totally different direction.

"I don't like Neil," I said softly. "Not in that way."

"But you asked him out," James pointed out.

"Yes, but . . ." I bit my lip. "It wasn't— I wasn't . . . there were other reasons I did it." I didn't dare say more.

"For whose benefit?" James murmured, almost to himself.

"What?" I asked, sliding nearer on the bench. I wasn't sure I'd heard right, and getting closer to James was a nice side effect.

"For whose benefit?" James repeated, louder this time, and looking straight at me.

For whose benefit? Why did that phrase sound so familiar? Where had I heard it before?

And then it hit me.

I hadn't *heard* those words.

I'd read them.

In *To Catch a Duke.*

It was what Lorenzo had said to Rosamund, during that last scene in the park.

I was losing my mind. There was no *way* James could be quoting from *To Catch a Duke.* I took a big, calming breath. The fact that he'd chosen the same words was nothing but a coincidence.

Then Francesca's words from last night sprang into my head: *There's no such thing as a coincidence.*

"Why did you say that?" I whispered.

For a second, James looked surprised, but

then his mouth curved up in that adorable half-smile that turned my knees to jelly.

"Because, 'If you love Alberto, I shall surely perish,'" he whispered back.

I really think my heart stopped in that second.

Frightened, I leaped off the bench and started backing away. "How . . ." I gasped, staring at James in horror. "How—do—you—know—that?"

Was James psychic? Psycho? Both? I held up my hands, wanting to keep him away. I had to escape.

James stood up too and walked toward me. "Norah, please don't freak. I'm sorry. I shouldn't have said it like that." He swallowed and ran a hand through his dark hair. "So I'm right, then? It was *To Catch a Duke* all along? The stuff you did—with the letter, and the flowers—it was from there?"

I opened my mouth but no words came out. I stopped backing up, though. Before I ran away, I needed an explanation from him.

Finally I managed to ask, "Did—did Audre tell you?"

James shook his head.

"Scott?"

"No."

"Nobody else knew!" I cried, panicked. "Did you sneak into my house at night and read my journal? You could be arrested for that, you know, and—"

James walked up to me and took my arm, which made me stop hyperventilating. "Norah, listen to me. Nobody told me. I didn't sneak into your house and read your journal. I read *To Catch a Duke*. That's how I guessed what you were doing."

"When did you read it?" I asked, noticing—in a good way—that James still hadn't taken his hand off my arm.

"One night in April—the night before Audre's party, actually."

The exact same night I'd read it. I don't believe in destiny, but I still got shivers all down my spine.

"*You* actually read Irene O'Dell?" I asked, more shocked by that fact than by anything.

James flashed his crooked grin again. "My sister. She's Irene's biggest fan. I always tease her about her giant collection of romance novels, and she always says I shouldn't knock them until I try them." He shrugged. "So, that one time, I did. Dina had just bought *To Catch a Duke* that morning, and she left it on the kitchen table after dinner. I stole it and—" His face colored.

I couldn't help but laugh, surrendering to the surrealness. "You liked it?" Obviously he'd liked it enough to memorize some of the lines.

"I stayed up all night reading it," James confessed (shivers, part two). "And . . . I got hooked. I knew the writing was bad and stuff, but it was still pretty interesting. It was kind of like reading *Cosmo*—getting to see the way a girl thinks."

"Guys read *Cosmo*?" This intrigued me.

James nodded, his ears going crimson. "*Cosmo, Marie Claire*, whatever. We'd never buy them, but, sometimes, if we think no one's looking, we'll, like, casually glance into one of them in a drugstore or something." He sighed and rolled his eyes. "I can't believe I'm giving away all these classified guy secrets."

"I won't tell anyone," I promised, laughing and momentarily forgetting my freak-out.

"It's the same deal with romance novels,

I guess," James added. "If your sister has a copy lying around—why not pick it up and see what's going on?"

If I'd known all these juicy truths about boys, I might have thought twice before putting the Rosamund plan into action.

"Okay, well, if it's confession time, here's mine," I began bravely, feeling calmer now that I knew James's story (his hand, by the way, was still on my arm). "I like to read romance novels too. In fact, I might be competing with Dina for the title of Irene O'Dell's biggest fan." I bit my lip, blushing.

James shook his head and (*no!*) took his hand away. "That's what tripped me up originally. At Audre's party, when I noticed you were holding the Shakespeare sonnets, and then when the whole love letter thing happened, it reminded me of Rosamund right away—since I'd just read *To Catch a Duke*. But then I thought: *What are the chances that Norah's read that book?*"

"Because I'm so serious about the book group books?" I asked. We drifted back toward the bench.

"Well, yeah. I mean, I am too, so I

admire that. Plus, I'd never believe that someone who loved Philippa Askance could also love Irene O'Dell."

Philippa and Irene. They represented the two sides of my personality, in a way. So it was like James was finally seeing who I *really* was.

"So, that first time, I just wrote it off as my own paranoia," James finished.

"But then . . . ," I prompted, still having heart palpitations.

"The meeting at your house." James grinned. "I thought I saw *To Catch a Duke* on your coffee table, though I wasn't sure. But by the time you got the double flower delivery—*and* said something about a Lorenzo, I was pretty much convinced. And when I saw you at the Angelika, that moment had Rosamund and Fitzgerald all over it. Everything matched."

It was so bizarre to hear James—in his familiar, wonderful James voice—talk about the characters I knew so well—and had imagined were somehow all mine. "And Neil matched Count Alberto, huh?" I asked with a sigh. There was no point in trying to cover my tracks now.

James rubbed his cheek, looking thoughtful. "Yes, and no. I have to admit, I—" He paused, and looked away from me again. "I did believe for a second that you really had a crush on Neil. That you guys were going to get together." He swallowed hard. "I was so, so jealous."

My heart soared but I didn't let myself get carried away—yet. "Jealous?"

James looked back at me. Slowly, he reached over and tucked a stray strand of hair behind my ear. I started to melt.

"Crazy jealous, Norah," he said softly. "Neil called me up on Wednesday to tell me about the date, but I acted like I didn't care either way. I guess I can be that way sometimes—it's like I hide how I really feel, even from my good friends."

I felt a sudden rush of bravery. "How *do* you really feel?" I asked breathlessly.

It was a question I should have asked him ages ago. If I had, then maybe I would have known sooner what James's fingers along my arm felt like. And then I'd have known what it was like to have him touch my cheek and feel my blood rush and boil.

James let his fingers trace the side of my

face, then drift toward the back of my neck. He undid my low ponytail, and my dark hair fell around my shoulders. My skin was suddenly so hot I didn't know if I could bear it. And, at the same time, I wanted more.

"How do I really feel?" James repeated quietly. "Can't you tell?"

I shook my head, dizzy. "Uh, I'm a little oblivious sometimes."

"Well, me too. Because even though I figured out *how* you did the Rosamund plan, I still don't understand *why* you did it," James said. "Was it really just to get my attention?" When I nodded, James moved his other hand to take mine.

Yes, really. James Roth was holding my hand.

"But you already had my attention," James murmured. "You had it from the first day I met you, at the meeting—just when I saw you. And then a little more when we had that psychic choosing-the-same-book moment. And then even more that night we talked at Art House. I almost didn't believe you could exist, Norah. Smart and well-read and funny *and* sexy? I thought that was only in books."

Was the level of my blushing potentially fatal?

James was silent for a minute, and I could tell he was working up his nerve. "By the way, you should know, you still have my attention," he added. "And . . ."— James swallowed hard—"my heart."

I promise you that's what James said. If I hadn't been slowly dying, I might have even giggled. Was he stealing lines from trashy romances too?

I know, I know. That's the moment I should have grabbed James Roth and kissed him like a madwoman. But I couldn't stop my stream of questions from spilling out.

"Why didn't you *act* that way, then?" I demanded (you will note, though, that I was still lacing my fingers through his). "You were always so distant after Art House, and that time with Philippa—you know, when you were going to—" I couldn't say the words "kiss me." Not yet.

"I'm a mess when I like a girl," James said, his ears going red. "I know that's a sucky excuse, but it's the truth, Norah. I get all shy and bumbly and weird and end up coming off like I hate her. And, since I like you more than I've ever liked any other girl—well, multiply that weirdness by one hundred. When we talked at Art House, it felt so . . . *real* that I got kind of freaked. The same thing happened when we were sitting in front of Philippa's house. I guess I *was* always pulling away from you, even though I wanted to be with you the whole time." James shook his head, looking troubled.

"It's okay," I assured him, grinning. "Clearly, I'm weird when it come to that stuff too."

"That's why I was so into the whole Philippa plan," James went on. "I mean, sure, I think Philippa Askance is awesome, but mostly it seemed like a good reason for the book group to stay together—for me to keep seeing you without actually having to ask you out."

So James, too, had had a scheme of sorts. And if that kind of confession can't make a girl—even a girl who's never been kissed—feel gutsy, I don't know what can.

I reached over, touched James's warm cheek, and gently turned his face back toward mine. He looked so little-boy vulnerable that I knew what I had to say.

"Kiss me," I whispered.

I watched, still not really believing this was real, as James leaned in toward me. There was his delicious vanilla scent, and the shape of his full lips, but now, suddenly, those lips were on mine. He tasted like strawberries and mint.

It was a warm, sweet, delicious kiss, one that would put Lorenzo to shame. Then I was kissing James back, and, surprisingly, I seemed to know what I was doing. We both did. James's hands cupped my face, and then my hands were in his hair, and the kiss kept on going, getting better and deeper and more intense the longer we kept at it. Kissing! How had I lived without it for so long? It seemed like the absolute best thing anyone could do with their time.

Only maybe that was just kissing James.

"So you *still* like me?" I murmured against James's mouth. "Even after you knew I was doing all the scary Rosamund stuff?" I hated to end that amazing kiss, but I needed to know. James pulled back slowly, his hands still in my hair, and he smiled.

"You can say that," he said. "If you don't believe me, maybe I should show you the, like, twenty poems I wrote about you, as evidence." I laughed, my heart singing, and he added, "Besides, people do crazy stuff for their crushes all the time."

I nodded. I'd had the exact same thought when Francesca had revealed her Neil scheme. Our whole book group, in a way, had done crazy things for love, from Griffin to Audre to, well, me, the craziest of all. I was about to tell James that, but then I realized that I could hold off. James and I had the whole summer in front of us to talk about crushes and the book group. And besides, maybe that had been our problem all along: talking. We spoke too much, using words as a way to cover up our truest feelings.

Sometimes, you need a break from words.

So, instead of saying anything else, I simply smiled, leaned in again, and put my arms around James's neck. And, finally, we stopped all our talking—and just kissed.

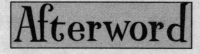

Afterword

Okay, yes. I'll be the first to admit it. I am now part of the kind of couple that used to make me gag on the subway.

James and I don't often make out in public, but we are—if I do say so myself—pretty adorable together (well, Philippa Askance said it too, so I'm really allowed). You can usually find us on a blanket in Prospect Park, reading; walking up and down Seventh Avenue holding hands; or sitting at a corner table in the Book Nook, sharing an iced latte while Audre sneaks us free cookies. Park Slope is even better when you get to share it with a boyfriend.

But here's the thing: I *may* be a romantic,

but I'm definitely not a hopeless one. I still hate cheesy pop ballads (although I did kind of choke up to "I Wanna Love You Forever" when it came on the radio the other day). I'm still happiest in vintage jeans (though sometimes I take Stacey's advice and wear a skirt). I still hate roses (though James did surprise me with the most perfect tiger-lily-and-lilac bouquet for my birthday in June) and boxes of chocolates (though I will make an exception when the chocolates are really, really good).

And, even after everything that happened with me, James, Rosamund, and Lorenzo, I still don't totally believe in soul mates, love at first sight, or destiny.

But I do believe in books.

Books are the reason James and I are together, and books are what will always connect us. And that's why, even though I'm finally living out the most blissful romance ever, I still find time to curl up with the latest novel by Irene O'Dell. Because boys are boys, and books are books, and, in the end, it's best to have a little bit of both.

LOL at this sneak peek of

Scary Beautiful

By Niki Burnham

A new Romantic Comedy from Simon Pulse

★

No one will admit it, but the first day of school rocks. Not the starting classes or getting loaded with homework part of it (please). It's the seeing everyone again part. It's getting all the gossip on who hooked up or broke up, who went on cool vacations to Maui (preferably sans parents) or had cat fights at sports camp. And—best of all— it's trying to predict which of the quiet, semi-invisible girls got a dye job, lost weight, or nabbed some fantastic summer gig in Paris and will therefore be angling to move into the "in" crowd.

My friends and I are always as hot to guess who'll be the year's surprise social superstar as my dad is to bet his retirement fund on whatever new-ish company he thinks will be the Next Big Thing on Wall Street.

Conversely, my friends and I also like to speculate about who'll fall on their face, becoming the pariah of the year. It's never a nice thing to see happen, but such is life.

This year, though, I'm too depressed to notice any of the usual first day of school maneuvering, even though everyone around me seems electrified with the possibilities of the year ahead.

The reason why is simple. Sean's not here.

Sean Norcross and I have been together since roughly halfway through eighth grade (okay, there's no "roughly" about it—it's been ever since he kissed me at exactly 7:48 p.m. on January 10, while standing in the snow in the parking lot after the school talent show.) So starting junior year with him all the way across the country sucks.

I mean, who in their right mind moves from Vista Verde, Colorado, all the way to New Haven, Connecticut, when they have three kids in high school? Well, that's just what Professor and Mrs. Norcross did. Sean's dad accepted a job teaching at Yale, since apparently the Ivy League's more fulfilling professionally than the University of Colorado. The Allied van left a month ago, headed east on I-70 with all the Norcrosses' furniture and at least a dozen boxes full of Professor Norcross's books on molecular biology. However, Sean, his younger brother, Joe, and his older sister, Darcy, were allowed to stay behind with their next-door neighbors for a couple weeks to finish up their summer jobs and tell everyone good-bye before they started at their uppity new East Coast private high school.

It sucked, seeing his house standing empty like that, knowing Sean was down to his last few days and would be following that bright orange moving van out of town.

Three days before he had to leave, Sean and I looked up New Haven on MapQuest and printed off the driving directions, just for kicks and giggles. I didn't tell Sean, but I wanted to do it just so I could mentally find my way there when I'm trying to go to sleep at night. It's exactly 1,867 miles from Vista Verde to New Haven, which MapQuest says should take only twenty-eight hours and ten minutes to drive. Even if that time includes bathroom breaks and stops for gas, it's a long haul.

Although counting miles is probably as good as counting sheep when I need to get myself to sleep, seeing that distance all plotted out on paper made me feel like I wasn't about to lose an appendage. Like I could draw a line from Point A to Point B and still connect with Sean.

Unfortunately, I was stupid enough to

think that Sean would want to try to make it work across that long distance too.

But no. Even if I *could* make that drive to New Haven, there wouldn't be a point. Because when Sean saw that map, it was like a switch flipped in his brain that said, "Babycakes, this relationship is *so over*." Our funky, cool connection, the one that enabled us to find each other instantly on a crowded football field or during a school assembly, no matter what else was happening around us, snapped just like that.

Only I didn't know it.

So this morning, instead of doing my usual people watching while I stand in junior hall, making mental notes about who's likely to make the cheerleading squad out of nowhere and who's going to wish they were invisible by the end of the month, I'm facing my new locker, messing with a combination lock that doesn't want to work, and I'm about two deep breaths away from tears. Everyone's staring at me as they walk past, and even though I'm used to people staring at me because of how I look, today I just don't want to deal.

I glance at the card with my new locker

combo on it again, then try to dial the numbers once more, wishing I could disappear inside my locker, just for a few hours, and stare at nothing but the cold, dark metal.

Then I realize that even doing that won't give me peace. If I get the stupid lock open, it's not like I can put Sean's picture in the back anymore without looking totally pathetic. At least, not once everyone learns that he dumped me cold while having breakfast at Pour la France in the main terminal of DIA, less than an hour before he hopped on the plane.

Who ends a relationship of two and a half years in an airport over scrambled eggs and French toast?

I feel Amy Bellhorn approaching before she speaks, and I will myself not to exude the aura of a red-eyed, horribly depressed dumpee.

"Chloe!"

"Hey!" I turn toward her, trying to sound equally excited. Since she's my best friend, I know how much she loves the first day of school—even more than I usually do. I give her a big happy-first-day-of-junior-year smile before focusing on my locker again. "What do you have first period?" I ask, sounding chipper enough to deserve an Oscar, given how I feel. "I'm in honors English."

"Mr. Whiddicomb or Mrs. Gervase?"

"Whiddicomb. You too?"

"Yep! This rocks. . . . We can catch up. So how'd things go with Sean before he left? Did Darcy and Joe give you any time alone together at the airport? God, you must be missing him like crazy already. I'd have called when I got my class schedule, but I knew you two wanted to spend as much time together as possible and then I was clothes shopping to get ready—"

"Thanks." I haven't told anyone about the breakup yet, not even Amy. I know I'll probably tear up the minute I say Sean's name, and I definitely will once anyone asks the *how did it happen?* question. No way do I want to go on a sniffly, ugly-ass crying jag on the first day of school.

I need to get myself to the point where I can talk about it, at least to Amy, without getting worked up before the first word even leaves my mouth, or else I'm going to be *the* topic of gossip today, and I hate being the focus of people's attention. It gives me the creepy crawlies, even when it's good attention that has nothing to do with my appearance, like when I get a high grade and the teacher puts it on the board, or when I make a killer return during a tennis match.

Amy puts a hand on my arm. "Hey, Chloe, you doing okay?"

Even though I mentally scream out *no*, I give Amy the best smile I can manage. "Okay enough. I think I just need to make it through this first week without him." Really without him.

"I'm here if you need to vent, you know."

I feel my jaw locking, so I just nod.

She apparently gets that it's time to change the subject as I give the lock a final, unnecessarily rough yank, because she tucks a stray strand of hair behind her ear, then pulls her schedule out of a notebook and holds it in front of her. "So let's compare. Who else did you end up with?"

I put a few items from my backpack into the empty steel locker, then pull out the schedule that came in the mail last week and hand it to her. "Pretty much everything I wanted. I ended up with Schneider for chemistry, though. Sixth period."

"Ouch. I managed to get Cooper. Fifth period. Apparently she's only teaching the one chem class this year too."

Lucky her. "That's when I have independent study. It was the only hour where Mrs. Berkowski could sponsor me, so I couldn't change it." I make a face. "Figures that's when Cooper would have chemistry. The one hour I can't be there."

It's not that one teacher's cooler than the other. Mr. Schneider just has a way, way tougher grading curve than Ms. Cooper and everyone knows it. Well, except college admissions officers, which is really the problem.

As we walk toward the gym, where they're having an assembly to update us on all the usual first day of school stuff, Amy stops walking and looks at me. "You know, you really look awesome, Chloe. Cleopatra exotic, you know? Especially since you were out in the sun and got a little more color."

I didn't take any extra time with my

hair or clothes today, even though normally I would have because everyone does on the first day back (whether they'll admit it or not), so I just shrug and keep walking. Amy falls in beside me. In an insistent voice, she adds, "No, really. I think you got even better looking over the summer. Like, scary beautiful."

"Oh, please. It's not like you didn't see me all summer. And I know what you're trying to do, so shut up already." I hear the "scary beautiful" thing all the time from Sean. Correction: *used* to hear it all the time from Sean. It was his phrase. I know she's using those exact words to try to make me feel better, but I really don't want to hear it now.

Besides, being pretty got me ostracized back in sixth grade for a while, even though Amy's probably forgotten all about it.

"Remember back when we were in middle school?"

I shoot her a look like, *What, you reading my mind?* but she continues: "On the first day of seventh grade? You hid out in the bathroom before homeroom because you got that awful haircut the day before and you didn't want anyone to see."

"Oh, yeah. Conveniently forgot about that." I told everyone how much I hated that haircut, then went to a different beauty shop the next night and had them recut it so I looked normal again.

What I didn't tell anyone—*especially* Amy—was that I got the bad haircut on purpose, over serious objections from my dad and the horrified stylist.

"Thanks so much for the memory, though," I say as we pass two panicked-looking freshmen. "I'm surprised you didn't take pictures."

"Oh, never," she says, all fake funny, because that's precisely what she did, threatening to publish them in our junior high school yearbook. It was her one and only foray into an organized activity that wasn't sports-related, and she got tossed off halfway through the year for skipping meetings so much. Needless to say, none of her work made it into the seventh grade section.

I wonder sometimes if it would have made things any better for me if she had gotten those pictures printed, just so people could see that I'm not always perfect, that

I'm not always pretty, and that I cry over stuff just like anyone else.

Probably not, though. Once people get an impression of you, it's hard to shake. I learned the hard way that getting a bad haircut to make yourself ugly—at least temporarily—isn't enough to do it. The whole episode just ended up making me feel worse.

As we enter the gym and scan the bleachers for open seats in the juniors' section, she says, "Well, I was just thinking things have changed since then, you know? And how it's a good thing you have a boyfriend, even if he is a zillion miles away. Otherwise, every girl in school would hate you based on looks alone."

Clearly, she doesn't know how much I *don't* want to remember middle school, or she would never say this to me. I mean, I know I'm not ugly, or even average. I have good hair, I'm tall, I don't gain weight easily, and I've never had a single zit. Not a one. It's not that I'm egotistical about it either. It's just a fact of life. A blessing of genetics. And, believe me, pretty girls *know* they're pretty, even the ones who are smart enough to be modest about it and pretend they don't know what they look like.

And I know why they do it. Let me tell you: Pretty sometimes sucks.